Barons Reach

Book 3
The Dreaming Series
by
Jan Reid

ISBN-10: 099445290X
ISBN-13: 978-0-9944529-0-0

Cover Image: Janaya Bird-Curtis (NEM) 2015 All Rights Reserved
Front Cover (source): Iandra Castle, NSW Australia.

Books by Jan Reid

Deep Water Tears
Book 1 The Dreaming Series

Grace
Book 2 The Dreaming Series

Barons Reach
Book 3 The Dreaming Series

DEDICATION

This novel is dedicated to those who keep 'The Dreaming' alive.

ACKNOWLEDGEMENT

Once again, I must first make mention of the incredibly inspiring NaNoWriMo challenge (National Novel Writing Month) in which participants are given the opportunity and encouraged to write the first draft of a 50,000 word novel between 1st November and 30th November.

Like - Grace: Book 2 The Dreaming Series, Barons Reach: Book 3 The Dreaming Series, is also a product of that challenge, and whenever I think of 'Barons Reach', I will remember NaNoWriMo (2015) with great affection. Thank you to all concerned.

My gratitude and sincere thanks again go to Wiradjuri elder Stan Grant (Senr), for authenticating and granting me permission to use the Wiradjuri content (dreamtime stories) in this novel.

My thanks also go to my very talented photographer daughter, Janaya Bird-Curtis (NEM), for kindly permitting me to use her wonderful photo of Iandra Castle NSW Australia, for the cover of Barons Reach.

AUTHORS NOTE

Although this is a work of fiction, I have endeavoured to ensure the authenticity of all Wiradjuri (Indigenous Australian) content through careful research and validation from Wiradjuri elder, Stan Grant (Senr), and in alignment with the book titled, 'A New Wiradjuri Dictionary compiled by Stan Grant (Senr) and Dr John Rudder'.

The name, Jimba, has been altered from the correct Wiradjuri spelling – Jiemba, although the correct pronunciation is the same as the altered spelling – JIM-ba.

The names, Binda, Jannali and Darel are the only non-Wiradjuri content. Binda and Jannali are believed to originate from the people of the Ngunnawal (NSW/ACT), and Northern Territory nations, respectively. The term 'aborigine' (as opposed to 'aboriginal'), is sometimes used for authenticity purposes. No offence is in any way intended by such usage.

In Chapter 3, the (part) account of the history pertaining to, 'The Bathurst War', Windradyne and the Wiradjuri people, was taken (and modified) from the (full) account at Wikipedia.

In Chapter 18, the story of the encounter between Windradyne and James Bartlett, and the 'Potato' incident, were taken (and modified) from the account at Wikipedia.

For information purposes, non-fiction content pertaining to the Wiradjuri peoples and Windradyne, has been added in the – Afterword, along with the Australian government's official, 'Apology to Australia's Indigenous peoples'.

Please Note: All content (other than mentioned above) is either a product of my imagination or used fictitiously. Any resemblance to actual persons, living or dead, locations or establishments is entirely coincidental, or has been fictionalised

'Those who lose dreaming are lost.'

– *Aboriginal Proverb.*

CHAPTER 1

Libby stops running and scans the emerald green paddock around her. She looks over at Jimba, an unspoken question in her glance.

"Where…" she begins, but Jimba is already pointing to the dam in the distance. They immediately hear the unmistakable yelp of a dog.

Libby takes off towards the noise, running faster than she has ever run before, but Jimba has already sprinted ahead of her.

Thoughts run wildly through her mind. Why hadn't Tiger come to her when she called? She had been calling him for the last hour. The black and white fox terrier had always come bounding back to her when she called – except…? She feels a sudden chill, even though the sweat is trickling down her face. Could it be the reason, why Tiger – yelped?

Libby is almost at the outer mound of the dam, but Jimba is already out of sight, having disappeared over it moments before. She reaches the top, misjudges the slope and slips on the pebbly dirt, falling hard on her bare knees. Tiger barks, and the stinging of broken skin, forgotten, as she looks towards the sound.

Her mouth opens wide in disbelief. Standing erect in the murky brown water, a huge kangaroo glares at Tiger. Tiger is up to his neck in the water, snarling at the kangaroo.

"Tiger!" Libby yells, but the dog is so focussed on the kangaroo he barely acknowledges her, casting only a glance in her direction.

She looks over to Jimba, closing in on the dog and kangaroo. He now calls to Tiger in an attempt to gain his attention, but he is also, virtually ignored. It is evident the dog has only one thing on his mind.

Panicking, her arms and legs shaking, Libby stands. It will be near to impossible to get Tiger to come to her now. Though only small, the fox terrier was the bravest of dogs - but he was also the most pig-headed.

Only last week, she had called her mother from the house to kill a brown snake Tiger had managed to coerce out of its hole. The dog had been intent on digging it out. Her mother had grabbed a shovel from the back of the house and within moments, she had chopped the snakes head off. She had then checked Tiger for any sign he had been bitten, while scolding him for his attack on the snake. Her mother had told Tiger he was too brave for his own good. The brown snake would have killed the small dog with one bite. But her mother wasn't here to save Tiger from a snake, or even - a kangaroo.

She shouldn't have even tried to persuade her mother to allow her to bring Tiger to Barons Reach. She had said Tiger would be able to warn her of any danger when she was outside playing with Jimba, and if he found a snake's hole, she wouldn't go near it. Instead, she promised she would run back to the homestead and tell Aunt Grace or Grandma Mary, as she had with her. It had worked. Her mother had finally given-in. She now wishes she hadn't. How was she going to get Tiger away from the enormous kangaroo he had now bailed-up?

Jimba has given up calling to Tiger. He glances at Libby, and begins looking earnestly around on the ground, his eyes darting from one place to the next.

Libby recommences calling to Tiger, her voice now almost hoarse from the last hour of yelling his name. But she can't give up. She has to keep trying...

Jimba spots what he has been looking for. He races over to the other side of the dam, away from Libby. He picks up a thick piece of broken branch and several medium sized stones.

Unlike the dog, the kangaroo had taken considerable notice of Jimba and Libby when they had both first appeared. But he hadn't seemed overly concerned when the two children were reasonably close together, further away, out of the water. The dog held most of his attention, anyway. However, now that Jimba has run over to the opposite side of the dam, he's beginning to feel a bit cornered.

He turns his head, glancing back and forth at Libby on one side of him and Jimba on the other. He makes a decision. He lurches forward, his paws landing on Tiger's head, and pushes him under the water.

"Nooooo," Libby screams, and runs to the water's edge.

"Get back Libby," Jimba calls out, and curses.

He doesn't usually curse around Libby. His father would be ashamed of him if he did. But he's frustrated now because his plan isn't going to work - so much for the idea of throwing the branch and stones at the dog. He knows better than to throw anything at a kangaroo, and especially one as big as this one. He's seen how powerful they can be, and he's now watching one try to drown a dog. He has to do something. He can't let this kangaroo kill his best friend's dog, and especially right in front of her eyes.

"Libby," he yells, "come here!"

Libby is too upset to take any notice. Sobbing, she bends down and grabs a handful of dirt in each hand. She then stands and hurls it with all her strength, although futilely, towards the kangaroo.

Jimba can see the tears pouring down her cheeks, now highlighted by the dirt she threw flying back into her face, and he can hear the despair in her voice as she repeatedly yells, "no, no, no…"

"Oh *hell,*" he mutters, pulls the piece of hardwood back behind him and throws it with all his might at the kangaroo. He's good at throwing, had plenty of practice, and he's the best thrower in his class at school. He hits his mark – the kangaroo's head, and the kangaroo immediately lets go of the dog and turns to face Jimba.

Tiger surfaces sneezing, but now subdued. Jimba breathes a small sigh of relief.

"Yeah, look at me," he yells at the kangaroo, with false bravado, although he avoids looking him in the eyes. That would constitute a threat, which the roo would feel the need to take on. However, he's not sure if it will make any difference now that he's basically attacked him. He forces himself not to think about it. He has to make sure Libby is safe, and the only way he can do that is to get that dog away from the kangaroo.

He notices Libby is now in the water, almost up to her knees, closing in on the dog. He's not out of trouble yet. He swiftly throws a stone close to the kangaroo to keep its attention, while Libby reaches forward and grabs Tiger. The kangaroo turns to look at Libby retreating with the dog, but decides Jimba is the bigger threat. He turns back to Jimba and moves closer towards him, sizing him up.

"Run Libby!" Jimba yells, and she takes off, the water splashing her pink shorts, turning them red. He's never seen her run as fast, even though she's now also carrying the weight of a small dog. He can hear her joggers squelching as she reaches the bank of the dam on the far side. He hopes she doesn't slip again. She doesn't, despite her sodden shoes, and disappears over the rise. He takes one last look at the kangaroo, turns, and sprints over the dam wall as well.

Rounding the dam, Jimba catches up to Libby and they slow their pace as they look behind them. They come to a stop when they see the kangaroo bound away on the other side of the dam.

Jimbo looks down at the dog Libby is holding tightly. "He's one lucky dog," he says, reaching over and patting the white patch on the top of his head, tugging gently at his black ears. Tiger responds by licking his hand.

"Oh Jimba, if it hadn't been for you…" Libby begins, looking despairingly into his dark brown eyes.

Jimba looks back into Libby's sky-blue eyes, now welling up with fresh tears.

"That's what friends do," he responds, with a wide smile, relief now evident that the danger has passed.

Libby sighs deeply as she blinks away the tears, and looks back down at the dog.

"I don't think I'll bring him again."

"Yeah, sounds like a good idea," Jimba agrees. "He's a goer, that's for sure," he says, rolling his eyes.

"Yeah, well - thanks," Libby replies, and her eyes now sparkle as she smiles softly. "You really are my best friend."

"Yeah, I know," he states confidently. "I wish you could be here more though," he says, looking across at the spire of the building behind the hills in the distance. He begins walking towards it.

Libby catches up to him, admonishing Tiger as he struggles to escape her tight hold. "No way am I letting you go Tiger. Be still. You're in big trouble."

"Hey, we better not tell anyone what happened," Libby says, looking sideways at Jimba.

"Yeah, no worries," he responds firmly. He had not been keen to tell his father about throwing things at the kangaroo, so he's relieved he's now off the hook.

Libby chews her bottom lip as she considers the repercussions of the adults finding out.

Aunt Grace might not let her play outside the house yard anymore - confine her to the house and garden. In truth, she could easily get lost exploring the house, and even the garden was a bit like a maze. She still hasn't seen both the inside or outside of the house, entirely yet; well, that she can remember anyway. She had only been a baby when she had first come to Baron Reach and she can't remember what she had seen then. If she were confined to the house and garden, she wouldn't exactly feel trapped, like she would at Binda, in her normal sized home near Dubbo. However, she would miss being able to roam wherever she wanted on the property with Jimba.

Aunt Grace's house at Barons Reach is a mansion, with more than thirty rooms. She tried to count them one day, when it was raining too much to go outside, but her legs got tired and she gave up her quest. At other times, she wandered around the house in awe at the huge rooms with ceilings that seemed to reach the sky, and strange old-fashioned furniture, like that double chair with seats facing opposite directions, those beds with big posts at each corner, and the thick, soft texture and rich, deep colours of the curtains, framing the windows.

Aunt Grace smiled at her when she asked her if she were a queen. She then pulled Libby against her in a hug, and said, "No, dearest, I'm just looking after this place for everyone."

That was when Libby had been five. Now, she was ten, and knew a great deal more.

Her mother told her that Aunt Grace's grandmother, on her father's side, once lived there, but she died, and now it was up to Aunt Grace to look after it. Libby replied that she didn't think it was fair that Aunt Grace had to look after such a big house all on her own. Her mother chuckled softly and said, "Don't worry, it's ok, Grandma Mary helps her a lot."

Grandma Mary was Libby's favourite person. Well, she reassesses, changing her mind, that's not entirely true. Including Grandma Mary, almost all her family were her favourite people; her mother – Rachel, and father - Darel, Grandpa Don, Aunt Grace, and even Uncle Dan. She doesn't see her Nana and Pop, her mother's parents, as much as the rest of her family, so perhaps that's why she doesn't include them as favourites. Her Pop gave great hugs, but her Nana seemed to make her mother mad a lot of the time, so maybe that had a lot to do with it. Libby doesn't like anyone upsetting her mother, including herself, although she admits that most of the time that was only because she doesn't like getting into trouble. Then there was her older brother, Will. He was also one of her favourite people, even though he annoyed her sometimes. However, he always helped her when she really needed it, like Jimba, her best friend. So they were included as her favourite people, too.

She looks down at Tiger wriggling in her arms. Yes, she was very lucky in so many ways. She would have been devastated if she had lost her favourite pet today, especially when he was her *only* pet.

If her mother found out what had happened, she would be certain to get into trouble. Her mother once told her that she reminded her of how she had been when she was little. She said she had also loved being outdoors more than anything, but at least she hadn't had a little dog leading her into trouble. She said there were enough dangers in the bush to be careful of as it was. Although she hadn't said it, Libby felt that the more times Tiger led her into danger, the more her mother regretted having bought him for her in the first place. She doesn't think her mother would ever give Tiger away, but she doesn't want to take the chance. Therefore, it is very important that her mother doesn't find out about the kangaroo.

Grandma Mary usually doesn't seem to worry about things as much as her mother, but she always seems to know what is going on too, before anyone tells her. Libby often wonders how she does that. She would have to do her very best to pretend nothing has happened today, when she is around her grandmother.

They push their legs to reach the top of the last rise where they'll be able to see the garden gate of the house, when Grandma Mary suddenly appears, walking towards them from the other side of the hill.

"So, here yous are," she says, scrutinising the faces of the blonde-haired, ten-year-old girl, and the ten-year-old boy sporting sand-coloured hair. "What have yous been up to?" she says, moving her eyes downwards from their faces, to the wet dog squirming to escape Libby's arms, her wet shorts and skinned knees.

"Nothin' Grandma," Libby immediately responds, guilt written all over her face. *Gosh, I have to do better than that*, she tells herself. "I mean, we were over that way," she says, motioning with her head towards the paddock where they had eventually found Tiger. *At least that part is true.* She praises herself for her quick thinking, and nods her head to confirm the truth of it.

"Hmm, well best be sure of ya story before you see Aunt Grace. She been mighty worried about you when you didn't come when she called," Grandma Mary responds, looking keenly at Libby.

"Ahum," Libby mumbles, and looks sideways at Jimba, biting her bottom lip.

Jimba looks down at his feet, hoping Libby's grandmother doesn't ask him any questions.

"No need to worry Jimba," Grandma Mary says, as if reading his mind. She turns to begin the walk back to the homestead with the two children in tow, adding, "I knows you would only be protectin' my granddaughter....*A lot of good that dog do at times*," she mutters, under her breath. "Come on you two, quick sticks," she says louder now, glancing behind her.

As Libby follows her grandmother down the hill to the garden gate, Jimba turns to follow the track to his modest home in the workmen's section of the property.

"See ya later," he yells, grinning at Libby, relief written all over his face.

Libby nods, smiling back, relaxing her grip on Tiger. He jumps from her arms and runs to Grandma Mary, looking up at her expectantly, a picture of innocence.

Grandma Mary looks down at him and shakes her head from side-to-side, knowingly. She opens the gate and ushers Libby and the dog through.

Libby turns suddenly and wraps her arms around her grandmother, burying her face in her soft cotton dress.

Grandma Mary rubs her back. "It alright child, you safe now. Best get you inside and clean up them knees, hey?"

CHAPTER 2

According to local knowledge, Barons Reach was one of the most well-known sheep and wool production properties in the Central Tablelands area of New South Wales, Australia, with a long history of ownership through the pioneering Bartlett family.

This local knowledge was backed up by historical records stating that in the early 1800's, Charles Bartlett staked his claim on 5,000 acres of prime land awarded to him by Governor Lachlan Macquarie, for successfully building a road over the Blue Mountains.

The town of Bathurst was established soon after; the oldest inland European settlement in Australia, positioned alongside the Macquarie River - part of the largest river system in Australia.

Over future generations, Bartlett and his descendants gradually acquired adjoining land, establishing tenant farming and several villages surrounding the town of Bathurst.

Therefore, by the time Grace Matthews (nee Taylor), inherited Barons Reach in late 1979, the land size of the property consisted of no less than 45,000 acres.

In recent years, new information about the homestead on Barons Reach became available to the general public, as just prior to the passing of Grace's grandmother, Old Mrs Bartlett, the home was added to the National Trust Register and the Australian Heritage Database.

The house, considered to be of extreme historical significance, recorded as being a Scottish, baronial mansion of Victorian Tudor style architecture, was comprised of granite and sandstone. Built in 1870, by James Bartlett, the son of Charles Bartlett, it replaced the original Georgian style building built by his father. The new building, named, 'The Manor', by James, befitting its size and style, was positioned on the highest of hills on the property, overlooking the vast Bartlett owned countryside.

However, after Grace arrived, the house was never referred to as, 'The Manor', again. Instead, it became known as, *the house*, by nearly everyone in the family, despite the new name engraved on a wooden nameplate that her brother, Darel, later fashioned and placed near the front door. Grace felt, nonetheless, that the act of renaming it had been a form of cleansing, particularly for her mother.

"So, how about we rename it – 'Murruway'?" Grace asked expectantly, after her mother translated the word 'path' into Wiradjuri for her. "It suits it, don't you think?"

"Yep, that sound real good to me daughter," Mary agreed without hesitation, and with a satisfied grin.

The reason for this name change held personal significance for Grace and Mary, and as Grace later predicted, for hundreds of people who passed through the front doors of the house in years to come.

"It wouldn't be right to rename the property itself though," Grace said, looking into her mother's eyes, hoping to see instant agreement about this topic there also. But when Mary's brow creased with a frown and she looked away, Grace knew this subject might prove difficult.

"Well, for one thing, remember the old diaries that described what happened during the Bathurst war and the night Windradyne came to this house?" Grace reminded her gently.

Mary nodded resignedly, but she wasn't ever going to leave it at that.

"Hmm, well it good to know the Bartlett's was good to the Wiradjuri people back then – respected them. Damn shame they didn't keep it up. That all I can say - Hmpf."

Grace placed a hand on Mary's arm and rubbed it tenderly, searching for the right words to soothe her.

Although Grace was twenty-two before she was finally reunited with her biological mother, there was now little she did not know about Mary's earlier life. Meanwhile, Mary was grateful that the little Grace did not know, was able to stay that way. She had decided there was more than enough sorrow in what she had already felt necessary to tell her.

Taken from her Wiradjuri family as a young child because her father had been white, Mary endured a heartbreaking separation from her family and way of life, in a Home for aboriginal children of mixed race. She was educated, trained as a domestic, and made to work in the local church. When she was considered old enough, she was released from the Home, and sent out to work at Barons Reach.

When her mother told her about her earlier life, it had been more than enough for Grace to find resolution for her own feelings of abandonment, especially with the revelation that she had been taken away from Mary and adopted out, the very same night she had been born at Barons Reach.

Mary had been forthcoming and honest about everything, except that which pertained to Grace's father.

She told Grace that she did not know the name of her father, and only that he had been one of the white workmen on the property, who had moved on shortly after finding a moment of comfort from loneliness with her.

However, when the truth later surfaced about her father's identity, a distraught and guilt-ridden Mary suddenly realized with great relief, that - all was not lost. Her daughter may now know who her father was, but she did not need to know anything about his true nature or the trauma involved with her conception. Her daughter could be spared the shame of knowing that, at least.

The truth, which Mary was relieved she could keep hidden from her daughter, was that Grace's father, John Bartlett Jnr, the only son of Old Mrs Bartlett, had raped her on the night she had been conceived, and he had continued to take advantage of her right up until the birth of her daughter.

When her pregnancy became apparent, Mary nervously told Old Mrs Bartlett that her son was the father. She should have known better, she later berated herself. It had always been the way of it, whenever a white person was involved and at fault. She had been accused of lying, and swiftly punished.

Mary knew Old Mrs Bartlett had known she had told the truth. How could a mother not know the character of her child, especially when that child still lived under the same roof? Besides, it often seemed the walls talked to the Mistress of Barons Reach. There was little she didn't know of that went on in her domain.

Old Mrs Bartlett had obviously fully prepared for the birth of Mary's baby. The clergymen had been lined up to take Grace as soon as she was born, and quickly dispatch her to a loyal church-going family, already chosen.

Mary had never known where Grace had been taken, and to ensure she would never find out, she had been quietly and efficiently put on a train to Dubbo, two days later, to a new employer, hundreds of kilometres away.

However, although stricken with grief and longing for her baby, the move to Dubbo literally became Mary's - Saving Grace. Though not a day passed that she did not think of her daughter and ache to hold her in her arms, Mary was to find her childhood home again, as well as her future husband. A husband who helped her to heal, gave her a precious son, and lovingly welcomed her long lost daughter into their lives, many years later.

"I know you don't like talking about her Mum, but she did leave Barons Reach to me, and she would have known I would find you; that you would become a part of Barons Reach too. After the way she treated us, well... perhaps she saw it as a way of absolving herself of the guilt, as well as ensuring someone with Bartlett blood remained at Barons Reach. Anyway, because we now have the responsibility of caring for the place where Windradyne rests, and the opportunity to help so many people, I think it would be best to leave the property name as it is. After all, we will be helping white people better understand the Wiradjuri ways too, so I think we need to compromise; leave the property name as Barons Reach, and just rename the house – Murruway, a 'path' for those seeking to find their way."

Mary nods again, but this time her dark brown eyes sparkle and her lips turn up in a soft smile. "Yes, you right! We need to show we can meet things half way. I so proud of you daughter. You got the right way of thinkin'."

From the moment Grace discovered the documents and old diaries in her grandmother's office in late 1979, she knew she had been given much more than an exceptional gift of property.

As she read the detailed events of 'The Bathurst War', a war which raged between the Wiradjuri nation, the largest aboriginal group in New South Wales, and the British colonists, in 1824, it became clear that she had been given a responsibility far beyond ensuring the ongoing prosperity of Barons Reach.

When she thought about her mother having lived and worked at Barons Reach, her own birth taking place under the roof of, The Manor, as it had been known as back then, and her subsequent inheritance of the very land it had all taken place on, it had all seemed to fall into place - the reason for it all.

Grace had felt greatly intimidated by Old Mrs Bartlett the day she had come looking for her mother, after discovering her place of birth had been Barons Reach. The old woman may have needed the assistance of a cane to walk, but there had been no other sign of weakness about her. However, although she had trembled slightly in her presence, Grace had held her own and met the formidable old woman's penetrating eyes with strong resolve.

At that time, Grace had not known that Old Mrs Bartlett was her grandmother, but her grandmother had known that

Grace was the daughter of Mary and her recently deceased son.

Grace had been shocked when contacted about her inheritance a few years later, after Old Mrs Bartlett died, and the truth of her father's identity, which Mary had withheld from her, was exposed.

When she later stood before the resting place of Windradyne, underneath an aging gum tree, on a grass covered hill at Barons Reach, she wondered...

Had her grandmother left Barons Reach to her purely because she had been determined to keep Barons Reach in the hands of the only living person with Bartlett blood, regardless of mixed heritage?

Or, had she considered, the Church of England, in Bathurst? Her grandmother had been a long and loyal supporter of the Church. She could have bequeathed Barons Reach to the Church if she had been intent on retaining white ownership.

Whether she had deliberated long and hard about it, or made an instant decision, Grace would never know. Though, in any event, Grace concluded, she would have known by choosing her granddaughter that she was returning the land to those with Wiradjuri heritage.

It had been clear in the letter Old Mrs Bartlett had written to Grace before she died, she had been devoted to Barons Reach. She had appealed to Grace, to ensure it would be well looked after.

She had also professed admiration for both Grace and Mary, while airing her disappointment in her deceased son.

Mary had not believed Old Mrs Bartlett's words had been sincere when Grace had read the letter to her. Grace had understood how difficult that would be for her mother, carrying so many sad memories as an employee of the old woman.

However, Grace believed she was able to read between the lines, and that her grandmother had sought to reconcile with both her mother and herself, even if from her grave.

Grace decided she would believe that was her grandmother's true intent, because what she envisioned for Barons Reach needed to be built on - reconciliation.

CHAPTER 3

"Following the crossing of the Blue Mountains in the early 1800's, and a flood of land grants given to the British colonists in the vast fertile lands in the Bathurst area, the British colonists put enormous strain on the traditional food sources and sacred landmarks of the Wiradjuri people. Unlike the pioneering Bartlett family, who maintained a respectful relationship with the Wiradjuri, and did not harm them in any way, many of the new settlers opposed the Wiradjuri people, even to the extent of attempting to exterminate them. The Wiradjuri were forced to fight back, and they were led by the Wiradjuri warrior and resistance leader – Windradyne, in what became known as, 'The Bathurst War'…"

Libby stands next to her grandmother as Aunt Grace reads from the document in her hands. She looks over at the old gravesite. The last rays of the setting sun touch the monumental metal plaque, and the light glints in her eyes. She squints and moves her head, attempting to escape it.

Grandma Mary looks down at her, distracted from listening to Aunt Grace, and puts a hand on Libby's shoulder to warn her to stand still.

Libby has heard the words Aunt Grace is speaking many times before. It was the same every time, although the people were different. She tries not to stare at them, and stand very still - with respect, as Grandma Mary has told her to.

She thought it strange that people have to come to Barons Reach to find out about stuff that happened so long ago. She asked Grandma Mary about it, one day.

Grandma Mary said the information was now available at other places too, but people liked to visit the gravesite of the leader of the Wiradjuri resistance of long ago. She said there were people from both white families and aboriginal families who wanted to know what really happened when the first white settlers arrived in the Bathurst area. She said there were always two sides to everything, but most people in Australia had only been taught one side of their country's history at school. She said that Aunt Grace had information most people had never heard about.

She understood what Grandma Mary meant about there being two sides. Her mother had often said she wanted to hear 'both sides of the story' when Libby had been fighting with her brother. Usually they both ended up in trouble because her mother said they should have compromised. She worked out that by *compromise* her mother meant she should meet her brother half way, come to some sort of agreement where although they both might not get everything they wanted, they would both at least get - something.

Grandma Mary also explained that people came to Barons Reach for different reasons. Some people came to find out more about the history of the area. Other people came because they wanted to learn about the Wiradjuri people who lived there for a very, very, long time before any white man even set foot in the area, or even Australia for that matter. Then, there were others who had family ties to the Wiradjuri people, but because they had been separated from their family by what happened all those years ago and even up until recently, they felt - lost. They were the ones who came because they were hoping to find something to help them not feel as lost anymore.

Aunt Grace has finished reading now. Some of the visitors stand silently looking at the gravesite, immersed in thought, while others blink away tears in their eyes. Then, as if on cue, everyone begins to walk quietly down the hill.

"Well, let's go then granddaughter," Grandma Mary says, and Aunt Grace catches up to them as they begin to saunter down the hill.

Libby likes the next part of the tour the best. After an early tea, they go to the big fire-site between Aunt Grace's house and the workmen's houses.

Jimba's father is responsible for setting up the fire for the story-telling. That means that Jimba is allowed to be there. She likes sitting with Jimba around the fire as Grandma Mary tells the Wiradjuri dreaming stories. Grandma

Mary said that when she was little, she used to listen to her grandmother tell them too. Libby thinks she knows all of them now, but she still likes to hear them again, and again. That way, she is sure she will always remember them.

Grandma Mary's father was white and her mother was from the Wiradjuri tribe from the Dubbo area, where Grandma Mary now lives. She says that makes her part aboriginal, even though she doesn't look like a lot of aboriginal people. She explained that to Libby to make her understand that she is also part aboriginal, like her father, Darel, Grandma Mary's son, even though she looks like her mother, Rachel, who has no aborigine blood in her family line. Libby liked it when she was told that because Jimba is also part aboriginal, although it wouldn't make any difference to her if he weren't. He is her best friend, no matter what.

Jimba told her that his mother was part aboriginal and his father is white. He said his mother told him that before she died. He said he wasn't sure what it all meant, until he came to Barons Reach. He said his mother told him that his name, Jimba, was an aboriginal name. The proper spelling was - Jiemba. She wrote it down for him on a piece of paper and he put it in a special box he's had ever since he can remember. He said it is his treasure box, full of special things, mostly about his mother. He told Libby that he reckoned his mother would have liked living at Barons Reach, but at least she would be glad he was here with his father.

Libby has been coming to visit Barons Reach with her grandmother ever since she was six-years-old. All of Libby's family live in the Dubbo area, even Aunt Grace. She is married to Uncle Dan. Uncle Dan works at the Dubbo Council. He has a very important job and he has helped Aunt Grace set things up at Barons Reach, so that lots of people can come to visit.

When Aunt Grace took over Barons Reach she straight away started setting things up for visitors to come and see the house and the old gravesite of Windradyne, and she even had lots of little houses, called cabins, built for people who wanted to stay overnight after the story-telling.

Aunt Grace does the house tours, and the reading of the history at the gravesite, and Grandma Mary does the story - telling around the fire-site, which was built especially for it, near the cabins.

Libby always gets excited when she overhears Grandma Mary telling her mother that Aunt Grace has bookings for visitor tours at Barons Reach, because that means she will be going with her. The bookings are usually on the weekends, but also at other times during the school holidays. She likes it when the bookings are during the school holidays the best, because Grandma Mary and Aunt Grace usually stay at Barons Reach longer then - sometimes for nearly a week, and she gets to stay too. Grandma Mary likes being at Barons Reach a lot, but she misses Grandpa Don, and Libby can tell that she is always really glad when they arrive home again.

At first, Grandma Mary used to go by herself to Barons Reach when Aunt Grace told her they had visitor tours booked. She would walk across from Jannali, the property where she and Grandpa Don live, to let Libby's mother know she would be away for a few days, and ask her to keep an eye on Grandpa. Libby's father usually saw Grandpa most days anyway, because they lived right next door on the neighbouring property, but Grandma Mary knew her mother would make sure he ate properly while she was away. She could have used the telephone to let her mother know, but Grandma Mary liked to walk along the track between the two houses. She said she needed to check up on the river now and then. Libby wasn't sure why she needed to check up on the river, because it always looked the same to her whenever she saw it, but Grandma Mary often said things she didn't understand.

One day Grandma Mary came to tell her mother she would be going away again the following weekend, and as she walked up the steps to the verandah, she overheard Libby complaining about not being allowed to go with her brother to help their father round up the sheep.

"How 'bout Libby come with me?" she asked her mother. "I'd suggest takin' Will too, but he seems to be happy enough taggin' along after Darel."

Her mother agreed to let her go, as long as she promised

not to give Grandma Mary or Aunt Grace any grief. So she had promised, and then been on her best behaviour for her mother. She had run all the way home from the front gate when the bus dropped her off after school on that Friday, to make sure she didn't miss out on going to Barons Reach with her grandmother. She hadn't needed to worry though, because Grandma Mary had been having a cup of tea with her mother, patiently waiting for her. When they arrived at Barons Reach that evening, they found that Aunt Grace had arrived only just before them. Grandma Mary said Aunt Grace must have left Dubba around the same time they were driving through it.

That first visitor tour had been so exciting. There had been so much to learn. But, the best part had been meeting Jimba. They had become instant friends.

The first time she had met Jimba, they had both been sitting around the fire like they were now, although not together. Grandma Mary had been telling the dreaming story about how the kangaroo got her pouch.

Libby now leans back, her arms outstretched behind her, as she sits cross-legged beside Jimba on a grassy patch near the fire. She wonders which dreaming stories Grandma Mary will tell the visitors tonight.

Libby watches Grandma Mary giving a dark-skinned lady a big hug. They separate and the lady moves away, dabbing at her eyes with a tissue. She then returns to the camp chair she had been sitting on before she went to speak to Grandma Mary.

Libby is used to seeing Grandma Mary hugging people. Some of them seem to get sad by visiting, but then they leave happy. Sometimes the visitors meet people they haven't seen for a long time and they end up crying and smiling at the same time. Grandma Mary does that a lot too, and sometimes on their way back to Dubbo, she tells Libby about some of the visitors that knew her family a long time ago. She has the biggest smile on her face when she tells her about them.

Grandma Mary finally sits down in a camp chair and looks around at the sea of faces watching her. She glances at Libby and they smile at each other briefly. Then she begins...

'This story is about a mother kangaroo, her baby Joey and an old wombat.

When the world was young, the mother kangaroo didn't have a pouch like she has now. Not having a pouch made it hard for her to look after Joey because as soon as her back was turned her baby would wander off exploring.

One day an old and grumpy wombat turned up. He kept complaining, over and over, about being weary and blind, and not having a friend in the world. When he told the mother kangaroo that he hadn't had anything to drink or eat for days, she felt sorry for him, even though he wouldn't stop grumbling. She told him she would be his friend and help him. She told him to hold onto her tail and she would take him to water and food.

So off they went, although it took a long time to get to where she wanted to take him, because the old wombat had trouble holding onto her tail. She had been very patient. But, by the time the old wombat was drinking and eating, she realised she needed to get back to Joey.

So she took off, and after searching high and low, she finally found him asleep under an old gum tree. She figured he was alright, so she bounded back to where she had left the old wombat to make sure he was still alright too.

The mother kangaroo was almost back to where she had left the old wombat when she sensed danger. Then she spotted a hunter moving close to the old wombat, so she made a lot of noise to distract him and led him far away, until the hunter finally gave up and went home.

By now, she was worrying again about Joey, so she bounded back to where she had last seen him, and with great relief found him still asleep under the old gum tree. She woke him and together they made their way slowly back to where she had left the old wombat. But no matter how much they searched they couldn't find him.

The reason they couldn't find the old wombat is because he had in fact been, Biyaami, the Creator Spirit, who had come down from the sky to test the kindness of his creatures.

The mother kangaroo was rewarded for her kindness. Biyaami presented her with a dilly-bag to tie around her waist, so she could carry Joey wherever she went. When she tied it to her waist though, the dilly bag magically turned it into a pouch.

From then on, Joey could be kept safe and she need not worry about him getting lost again; she could take him with her wherever she went.'

Libby and Jimba look at each other as soon as the story is finished. They exchange a knowing look as the people start talking around them.

"That big kangaroo today wasn't very kind to Tiger though, hey," Jimba says, flatly.

"Yeah, I reckon," Libby replies.

The mention of it makes her see the image of Tiger's head being pushed beneath the water by the kangaroo. She sighs deeply and shudders.

Jimba notices, and he looks briefly at his friend's sad face. He hadn't meant to upset her. He quickly changes the subject.

"Hey, that story was the one we heard when we first met, remember?"

Libby nods, and a smile returns. She notices the people have stopped talking because her grandmother has just told them that the Wiradjuri name for kangaroo is - *wambuwany*. Some people attempt to repeat the word, especially some of the children. Grandma Mary waits for them to quieten, so she can begin another story.

Libby thinks of some other Wiradjuri words Grandma Mary has taught her; *gadi* – snake, *gugubarra* – kookaburra, and *garang* – land.

She watches Jimba pick up a stick beside him. He starts to draw with it in a small patch of dirt, as they both listen to Grandma Mary begin her next dreaming story.

He has drawn two stick figures with big smiles on their faces. One stick figure has long wavy hair, so she is sure it's meant to be her. The other one is without a doubt, Jimba. She knows with certainty because it has short hair and it is much taller than the other one. Trust Jimba to point that out, she thinks. She is trying hard to catch up to him, be as tall as he is. They are the same age, after all. But, she's not annoyed at him. She can't imagine anything coming between their friendship, and she has no doubt that Jimba will be her best friend - forever.

CHAPTER 4

Libby catches a glimpse of herself in the mirror on the wall, as she struggles to hold onto the box she carries down the hallway to her bedroom. She grimaces. Her long blonde hair is a mess of tangles from leaving the windows down as she drove out to Binda and back.

She is glad Teagan isn't home. It would just give her another excuse to badger her about letting her cut it so it would be more manageable. How she ended up close friends and sharing a unit with a hairdresser, she will never know. They couldn't be more different.

She reaches her bedroom and nearly topples over on top of the box, as she lets it slip from her hold onto her bed. The box tips over spilling books and a photo album onto the floor. She restores her balance and bends down to pick up the books, and lastly, the photo album. She notices a photo falling out and pulls it out to look at it.

She sits on her bed as she looks at the photo. She is standing beside her childhood best friend, Jimba. He is smiling at the camera, but it looks like a forced smile; it doesn't quite meet his eyes. She is looking down at Tiger and reprimanding him for not standing still. The photo had been taken just after he had jumped up on her.

She remembers Aunt Grace taking the photo. She took it the morning of the last day she was there.

Grandma Mary had taken her home the next morning, and she has never been back.

Sadness grips her as she continues to look at the photo. She could never have gone back to Barons Reach after what Roger had done, and all the repercussions from it.

She touches two of her fingers to her lips and places them on the image of Tiger, and the memory of that day, over ten years ago now, plays in her mind, as if it were only yesterday…

Jimba was waiting for her at the garden gate, like he usually was. But, he looked distracted that morning. He kept looking back over his shoulder. She hadn't had a chance to ask him why, because Aunt Grace had followed her outside. She said it was about time she had a photo of them together. And Tiger, she added. She asked Jimba to come into the house yard and stand next to Libby in front of the purple Wisteria hedge.

Libby remembers how she had been looking forward to that day. The last visitor was to leave that morning and she had the whole day to spend with Jimba, without the need to attend any more tours. Grandma Mary said to make the most of it, because they would be leaving to go back home the following morning.

They had planned to go to their secret place, their makeshift cubby house they had built around the big ghost gum over on the next hill. They would climb the tree through the hole in the roof of their cubby house and sit idly in the branches looking out at the surrounding countryside, keeping an eye out for any trespassers, searching for anything they thought looked interesting.

They once saw a baby Magpie fall from its nest in the next tree. They scrambled down the ghost gum and through the cubby house to look at it. It hadn't looked like a black and white Magpie at all, but they had watched its parents flying in and out of the tree earlier and they knew it couldn't be anything else. With wrinkled grey skin covering protruding bones, it looked downright ugly. But Libby had felt sorry for it, watching it wriggle and squirm and cry out with pitiful noises. She knew she would have trouble holding it though, because of the way it looked. Besides, she wouldn't be able to climb up the tree with one hand to return it to its nest. However, she didn't want to just leave it there though, defenceless, on the ground. Jimba had known he would be the one to return it to its nest. He was a better climber than Libby anyway. He gently scooped up the bird in his hand and placed it in a type of sling he made with his tee shirt. Then, after Libby gave him a leg up so he could reach the first branch of the trunk of the tree, he slowly made his way up to the nest.

When he came back down he said there were another two baby birds in the nest, but they looked much bigger. They had both felt proud of themselves for rescuing the bird. But later that day, they saw it fall out again, although this time one of the parent Magpies was in the nest. They waited expectantly for the parent bird to fly down to its baby, but it just flew away. They scampered over to the little bird and saw that it was dead. They then buried it at the base of the tree, with great care.

When Libby told Grandma Mary about it, she explained that the parent may have smelt their human scent on it, and rejected it.

Libby was horrified that although they had tried to help it, they may have ended up causing it to die. Grandma Mary must have known what she had been thinking, because she then told Libby that the parent bird could also have rejected it because it had known the baby bird was too weak to survive.

"It no good being weak granddaughter. Nature show us that. You gotta be tough to survive in life."

As soon as Aunt Grace went back into the house after taking the photo, Jimba looked back out over the gate. She looked where he was glancing, but she couldn't see anything. She was about to ask him why he kept looking there, when he began to speak, words spilling out.

"Roger will be here soon. The Manager's nephew. Dad said I have to let him come with me. Help him settle in here. I wish I didn't. He's, well…I…don't like him very much."

And before Libby could reply, their attention is drawn to the sound of the gate latch, opening and closing. A tall, dark-haired, lanky boy, leans back against the closed gate, wearing a smug expression.

"So, who we got here?" he asks, as he looks Libby up and down, raising his eyebrows."

Before Libby can say anything, Jimba replies defensively. "This is Libby. Her aunt owns this place."

Roger turns to the Wisteria hedge alongside the gate and grabs a piece of the green foliage with purple flowers, ripping it off with a quick tug. He looks down at Tiger standing beside Libby and begins to throw pieces of it at the dog. Tiger growls.

"Is that your mutt?" he asks, glancing at Libby while glaring at the dog.

Intimidated by Roger's tall statue towering over her, and annoyed by his words, Libby unconsciously pulls herself up, to stand as tall as she can.

"That's Tiger, and yeah, he's my *dog*." She emphasises, showing her displeasure at his reference to Tiger as her 'mutt'.

Roger laughs mirthlessly and throws the remaining Wisteria aside as he moves away from the gate, closer to Libby.

"Well, ya better keep him under control, 'cause if he bites me he'll regret it," he threatens.

Jimba has been watching the uncomfortable exchange between Roger and Libby, concern written all over his face. He needs to talk to Libby, away from Roger, but he doesn't know how he's going to manage it. However, at this moment, he knows he needs to get Roger's attention away from Libby.

"Race you to the river...," he says, looking decisively at Libby, and makes his way out of the garden. He stops on the other side of the gate, waiting...

Libby decides she has had more than enough of Roger already, and wants to get as far away from him as possible. She bends down and pets Tiger.

"Be good," she whispers.

She makes a move towards the gate, but pauses and looks at Roger, to indicate she wants him to leave.

"That mutt coming too?" he asks.

Tiger growls again and Roger grins at him malevolently.

"*No!*" Libby says adamantly, and she stares at Roger with contempt.

With a nonchalant shrug, Roger moves in front of Libby, opens the gate and walks through.

Libby follows, and she pulls the gate towards her, the latch clicking as it closes.

Jimba and Libby exchange glances, and by mutual agreement they begin to run towards the river. They look over their shoulders to see Roger sauntering behind, watching them.

Libby remembers how they both made it to the river well ahead of him and they immediately began talking as they caught their breath.

"He's… horrible." Libby begins first.

"Yeah, I know." Jimba replies with a grimace.

"Why does he have to be with you? I mean, he's gotta be a lot older for a start."

"Yeah, he's fourteen. Mr Sutton is his uncle. Mr Sutton came over last night after the story-telling. Dad sent me to bed then, but I heard them talking outside. Mr Sutton told Dad he wants me to show him around the property, get him used to the place. He said something about him being in a bit of trouble in Bathurst and that his mother, Mr Sutton's sister, is hopin' Mr Sutton can straighten him out. He'll be catching the same school bus into town with me too."

Libby bites her bottom lip, deep in thought.

"So, he could be here for a while then?"

"Yeah. Mr Sutton told Dad your aunt said it was ok."

Jimba picks up a stone in the pebbly dirt, walks closer to the water and half-heartedly throws it into the river.

They both immediately turn towards the bushland they have come from, when they hear twigs snapping.

Roger appears and saunters down to the river with a thick long stick in his hand, ignoring them both. He gazes across the water to the bank on the other side.

"So what do you do around here for kicks?" he says to no one in particular.

Libby and Jimba look at each other quickly, and by silent agreement, they know they're not going to tell him about their secret cubby house.

"We find things to do," Jimba replies, still looking at Libby.

"Like *what*?" Roger snaps, and turns to look at them.

"We explore and sometimes go swimming," Libby responds.

"Ok then," Roger says with a glint in his eye, and in two long strides he is behind Jimba, shoving him towards the water."

Libby rushes towards Jimba as he stumbles and splashes at the water's edge, but he regains his balance, and glares at Roger."

"You're so meeaann," Libby yells, looking at Roger angrily.

"You're so meeaann," Roger mimics Libby, and sniggers. "You want to go for a swim too," he says, taking an exaggerated step towards her.

Libby back steps away from him quickly, panic in her eyes.

"Aww, you two are just little kids," he says, and begins walking away, swinging his stick. "I'll go make my own fun." And with that, he disappears into the trees.

Why hadn't they believed her? She knew Roger had killed her dog. She had shut the gate when they had left that morning. After Tiger had nearly been killed by the kangaroo at the dam, she wasn't going to let him out of the house yard again. And she wasn't ever going to bring him back to Barons Reach.

When she went home at lunchtime, the gate was wide open and she couldn't find Tiger anywhere in the garden. She raced into the kitchen where Grandma Mary and Aunt Grace were preparing lunch and asked them if they had seen him. They both said they hadn't left the house yard that morning.

Aunt Grace told Libby that she probably hadn't shut the gate properly when she left earlier. But she had made sure she had, especially after Roger had threatened Tiger. And Aunt Grace and Grandma Mary didn't know about the kangaroo incident, so they didn't understand why she was so worried about Tiger getting out.

"Don't worry sweetheart, he's bound to show up. He's probably just exploring. I bet by the time you finish your sandwich he'll be back." Aunt Grace said, gently turning her around and pushing her towards a chair at the table.

But Libby remained standing once Aunt Grace's hands left her back, and she looked across the table at her grandmother, imploringly.

"Roger's let him out. I know it Grandma. Tiger growled at him and he was really mean to Tiger," she claimed, as tears began to stream down her face.

"Who's this Roger fella? Grandma Mary suddenly asked, looking at Aunt Grace with a frown.

"Oh, he's Bill's nephew. He'll be staying for a while."

Grandma Mary looked back at Libby, deliberating, and then made a decision. She turned her attention once more to Aunt Grace.

"I'm goin' for a walk…" she began, quickly walking around the table towards the door, "…see if I can find this dog. Best put Libby's sandwich on hold," she added, as she stopped and turned her head to look at Aunt Grace again. "You not gunna get her to sit here and eat while she so het up."

Libby immediately raced over to her grandmother, relieved that at least someone had finally taken her seriously. Aunt Grace then offered to go with them to search, but Grandma Mary said there was no need. Libby would go in one direction and she would go in another. She said she would find the dog. And she did!

Libby had taken off in the opposite direction to her grandmother, as planned, calling to Tiger over and over. But after a few minutes, her throat became sore, so she stopped to listen instead. When she had heard a noise, she strained her ears, hoping to hear the familiar bark of her little dog. Instead, she deciphered her grandmother calling. But not to Tiger. She was calling to Libby. She had held her breath for a few seconds, hope welling in her chest. *Grandma Mary must have found him.* She ran full pelt back to the house yard, remembering that they had arranged to go straight back to the house yard if either one found him.

Grandma Mary said she found Tiger lying on the ground near an old gum tree. She said there was a big old branch that had fallen off the tree right beside him. It looked like the branch had fallen on Tiger's head. He most likely never felt a thing, her grandmother said quietly, as she gently placed the dog on the grass in the garden.

Between sobs, as she sat on the grass petting her dog with shaking hands, Libby told Aunt Grace and Grandma Mary that Roger was trying to make it look that way. He had killed Tiger with a stick he had been carrying around. She just knew it. Her aunt and grandmother had looked at each other, but neither one said anything.

Jimba turned up as Aunt Grace was digging a small hole in the corner of the garden, near the yellow rose bush. He had heard voices when he had arrived at the garden gate, and headed towards the sound.

Grandma Mary was standing beside a tiny black and white bundle that he instantly recognised.

Libby spotted Jimba approaching, and ran to him.

"It was Roger…he *killed* Tiger… I just know he did," she sobbed, tears streaming down her face.

Jimba's eyes began to well up with tears seeing Libby so distraught, and at the news about Tiger, but flickers of anger kept them from falling.

'But, they don't *believe* me," Libby added, whimpering, and looking beseechingly into his eyes.

Jimba was torn. He wanted to tell Libby's aunt and grandmother that he could easily believe Roger had killed the little dog also. But he didn't know for certain, hadn't actually seen him do it.

If he said anything, Libby's aunt might tell Mr Sutton, and then, Mr Sutton might tell his father. Mr Sutton and his father both expected him to help Roger settle in, and if he accused him of killing Libby's dog, when he hadn't, well, that wouldn't be good at all.

Mr Sutton and his father got on really well, but if it came down to it, Mr Sutton would more than likely take his nephew's side. After all, he was family. His father had taught him to always tell the truth. If he were wrong about Roger killing Tiger, he would be letting his father down, especially if he backed him up against Roger, like he probably would.

If he caused any problems between his father and Mr Sutton, they might have to leave Barons Reach. No, he couldn't let that happen. He didn't want to live anywhere else, and if they had to leave, he might never see Libby again.

So, the two ten-year-olds gave the little dog a final pet and then stood side-by-side as Grandma Mary gently placed Tiger into the hole in the ground. Aunt Grace then covered him with the loose dirt.

Libby couldn't understand why Jimba didn't say anything to her aunt or grandmother. It made her so mad. Why wasn't he backing her up?

When Aunt Grace walked away to return the shovel to the shed, Grandma Mary watched the two children, thoughtfully, as they walked towards the garden gate.

Libby felt drained from all her crying, and she was now confused. Jimba had remained silent about Roger, and she felt he had let her down. She decided she was going to have a go at him about it as soon as they were far enough away from Grandma Mary.

They were almost at the gate and Libby was about to speak, when Roger appeared.

"Aww, what's the matter little girl, something happen?" he asks, with his now familiar, smirk.

"Go away!" Jimba replies instantly, glaring at Roger.

"Well, I told you I'd take care of that mutt if he bit me," Roger replies flatly, and ensuring he has Libby and Jimba's attention, he leans down and pulls up the leg of his tattered jeans. Bright red teeth-marks leave no doubt they are Tigers.

As the two children stare, struck dumb by the callous confession, backed up by indisputable proof, he lets go of the material, smiles mockingly, turns and walks off chuckling, swinging the long stick he had been carrying earlier.

Libby is the first to regain her senses. She turns and glares at Jimba. He knows she was mad at him earlier for not saying anything to her aunt or grandmother, and she's now - furious, because Roger's confession has just proved she had been right. He doesn't blame her, one bit for being angry with him.

"Granddaughter?" Grandma Mary says firmly, from the verandah behind them.

Libby and Jimba both turn towards the verandah.

"Come with me granddaughter! Jimba, off you go now," she says more gently.

Jimba opens his mouth to say something, but Libby ignores him and races up the steps to her grandmother. With a last look at them walking away, he walks dejectedly out the gate.

Aunt Grace still didn't believe her when once again she told her and Grandma Mary that Roger had killed Tiger; that he had actually *told* her and Jimba.

"Oh sweetheart, perhaps you misunderstood what he was saying? Tiger may have bitten him, but I can't imagine Roger harming him. His uncle said he's had a bit of a rough time the last few years. Maybe he was trying to act tough because he could tell you don't like him. And, it's not unusual for an old gum tree to drop its branches at any time. It was just rotten bad luck for Tiger. I'm sure you're just not thinking clearly at the moment. It's been a big shock."

Grandma Mary didn't say anything after that, as she rocked Libby in her arms until she finally stopped crying. However, as soon as Aunt Grace left them alone, sitting on the soft cushioned verandah chair, looking out across the green expanse before them, she said quietly, "Some people real mean granddaughter, but if you let that meanness soak into your bones, it mighty hard to get rid of. Don't let that meanness soak into you, you hear! That the way to show 'em they lose. Let it go granddaughter."

Libby knew Grandma Mary believed her then, and she had nodded her exhausted head, sighed deeply, and fallen asleep, cocooned in her grandmother's warm arms.

***

Libby hears a noise at the front door of the unit, and recognises the jangle of Teagan's bangles as she places her keys in the dish by the door.

She puts the photo back inside the photo album and places it on the bed.

Teagan appears at her bedroom door.

"Hi," she says, chirpily, but a concerned look suddenly appears as she meets Libby's eyes. "Are you ok?"

Libby realises that her hair is still a mess, but she can feel teardrops tickling her lids. That is what Teagan has probably noticed. She must have been so absorbed in the memory, she hadn't realised she had been crying.

"Yes, I'm fine," Libby replies, wiping the moisture from her eyes with her fingertips, quickly composing herself. "I've just been looking through some old stuff I brought back from Binda."

"Ok then," Teagan says, although she doesn't look at all convinced by her words. "How about a cuppa?" she asks, and without waiting for a reply, turns around and begins walking back down the hall towards the kitchen.

"Ta, sounds good," Libby replies, knowing that Teagan will still hear her.

Determined to cast aside her sad reminiscence of Jimba, Tiger and Roger, she gets up from her bed and reaches for her hairbrush. *Looks like I got off this time*, she thinks, managing a small chuckle.

"You know Libby, you really should let me do *something* with your hair," Teagan yells from the kitchen.

Libby rolls her eyes and continues brushing.

CHAPTER 5

Libby tosses and turns in her bed. Try as she might, sleep evades her. If only she could stop thinking about Barons Reach. She knows she has no one but herself to blame. If she hadn't decided to bring back that box from her bedroom at Binda, she wouldn't have seen that photo that Aunt Grace had given her, and been reminded.

She had just wanted to bring back a couple of her favourite books to read again, but instead of looking for them specifically, she had brought back the box she knew she had put them in before moving into town to Aunt Grace's and Uncle Dan's.

In March 2002, a few months after finishing her Higher School Certificate at Dubbo High School, she began working for the Dubbo Council. Of course, Uncle Dan had had a lot to do with that. But she had worked hard at the clerical position in the Environmental Services division of Dubbo Council, wanting to prove that she was worthy of the job on her own merits. And the last two years had proved it, even though she was the niece of Dan Matthew's, the Director of Community Services.

She could have driven to Dubbo each day to work, in the red Mazda 323 hatchback she had received as an eighteenth birthday gift from her parents in February. However, that would have entailed a fifty minute trip, each way, to town and back home. Aunt Grace said she couldn't see the sense in that, when she could easily board with them.

With her car packed with her clothes and some personal items, she drove away from Binda, the 3,000 acre wheat and sheep property, in the Central West Slopes and Plains of New South Wales, a few days before beginning her employment at Dubbo Council.

Grandma Mary had turned up at the house at Binda as she had been packing the last items into her car, she had decided to take with her to her aunt and uncle's. Libby had walked over to Jannali the day before, to say goodbye to her, but Grandma Mary had decided she wanted to be there to wave her goodbye, and to remind her…

"Now, don't forget granddaughter, you can still come home on the weekends to see us. We not goin' anywhere."

Her mother told her that she would miss her too, even though she saw the practicality of her boarding with her aunt and uncle, and encouraged Libby to accept their offer.

However, even though she was grateful for her aunt and uncle's kind and very helpful offer, she was hesitant at first to accept it. The reason she was hesitant though, had nothing to do with how she felt about Aunt Grace or Uncle Dan, or even leaving her family home.

Aunt Grace was always kind to her. She had once even told Libby that she wished she had a daughter just like her. Even though she was very touched by her aunt's words, it had also made Libby feel a little sad for her, especially when she found out that she had wanted to have children but hadn't been able to. She was a lovely aunt and Libby thought she would have been a wonderful mother.

Uncle Dan would have been a great father too. He was always making jokes and Libby laugh - away from work, anyway. At work, he was a bit more serious, but he was always very helpful, and had a smile for her if he happened to walk past her workstation.

The reason she didn't immediately accept her aunt and uncle's offer was because she suddenly felt guilty about not having returned to Barons Reach over the previous eight years. It was something that seemed to raise its head from nowhere.

She had previously felt that her reasons for not returning to Barons Reach had been entirely valid, so she found it difficult to understand why her conscious had started to bother her.

After all, Roger had killed her dog, Aunt Grace hadn't believed her, and Jimba had let her down. And, on top of all that, her little dog was lying in a grave in the corner of the garden there. Why would she have wanted to return and be reminded of all those things?

She hadn't wanted to be mad at Aunt Grace for not believing that Roger had killed her dog. She had tried really hard to understand why she hadn't believed her. She had never lied to her aunt – *ever*. So she couldn't help but be mad at her for not believing her, especially while the initial heartbreak of being without Tiger had been so raw. Until, eventually, she began to think a little more clearly...

Aunt Grace hadn't known what Roger was really like. She had most likely only agreed to let him stay at the property because he was Mr Sutton's nephew. Aunt Grace always seemed to get on well with Mr Sutton, the Property Manager of Barons Reach. She had often noticed them conversing when she visited. Mr Sutton was always very polite to

Aunt Grace and Libby remembered her nodding her head while he was talking to her, and smiling at him when their conversation had finished.

He had also been very nice to Libby and Jimba. She remembers the time she and Jimba had left a gate open, and several sheep escaped from the paddock. Mr Sutton found them in their cubby-house and asked them if they had been over that way, and left the gate open.

Libby and Jimba had immediately looked at each other, and their guilt had been obvious. So, with solemn faces, and each apologising, they admitted they had left it open, wondering how much trouble they were about to be in.

However, instead of rousing on them, as they had thought he would, Mr Sutton had just reminded them that it was very important to abide by the law of the land – if a gate was open, you left it open, but if a gate was closed, you always closed it after going through.

He didn't tell Aunt Grace or Jimba's father on them either. Instead, he just asked them to help him round the sheep up and return them to the paddock. Libby had actually really enjoyed it, so even though she didn't feel it was much of a punishment, she never forgot to abide by the law of the land again.

Libby eventually accepted that Aunt Grace probably couldn't have imagined for a moment that Mr Sutton's nephew could be as mean and cruel as he had been. When she had finally arrived at that conclusion, she found she didn't feel even the slightest bit mad at her aunt anymore.

Her feelings had changed little about Roger though. She had never imagined she could hate someone as much as she had hated Roger. She was still trying to come to terms with what he had done, all these years later. Her grandmother had told her that it wouldn't do her any good to hold on to that hate, or meanness, as she had called it. Well, even if she were to try, how much less hope would she have of letting it go, if he were still around Barons Reach when she visited? Staying away from Barons Reach was the only way she could see any possibility of ever being able to find any semblance of peace about what he had done.

As for Jimba, well, she missed him, but every time she started to even consider the possibility of going back to see him, she reminded herself of how she had felt towards him that last day. They had been best friends. How could he have *not* said anything? Their friendship could never have been the same again. Besides, she wanted him to know that she was still mad at him for his disloyalty, and again, the best way to do that was to stay away.

By the time she had returned to Binda she had felt completely emotionally exhausted from all that had happened, and with her Aunt's words that she must have been mistaken about Roger, still ringing in her ears, she imagined she would probably have received the same doubtful responses from her immediate family. They hadn't met Roger. They didn't know what he was like. She just couldn't bear to hear the same conclusions from them. She had just wanted to feel their compassion, as she had from her grandmother, not be riled up in protest at their unbelief. So she didn't tell them that she knew Roger had killed Tiger, and her mother, father and even her brother, Will, comforted her with their loving sympathy at the loss of her dog.

A few months after she had last been at Barons Reach, her mother asked her if she would like another dog. She would never forget that moment. She had looked at her mother's kind eyes and instantly known that although she had sometimes complained about the little dog, and had even had to protect her daughter when the little dog had led her into dangerous situations, she missed him too. But she just couldn't bring herself to even think of loving another dog, and have it taken away from her because of some unforeseen event. She had learned about loss through losing Tiger, and she knew the heartbreak it brought.

She decided the best thing would be to try to forget about everything associated with Barons Reach. 'Out of sight, out of mind,' was a phrase she had heard her mother say, and Libby felt it suited her situation, perfectly. She embraced it, as best she could, and began spending more time with some of her other friends at Barwon Primary School, the little rural school she attended close to Binda.

By the time she started Dubbo High School a year later, she had become so caught up with new friendships she made there, she often didn't think of Jimba, for even days at a time. Whenever he came to mind, she would make herself think of something else.

Aunt Grace brought up the subject of Barons Reach to her a few months after that last day she had been there. She told her that Jimba always turned up asking about her whenever she went back for a tour. She said it was obvious he was missing her. Libby responded with a nod of her head, but her feelings were still quite raw and she hadn't known what to say, so she remained silent. After that, Aunt Grace never mentioned Barons Reach to her again.

Likewise, although it seemed Grandma Mary made a point of looking her way when telling her mother every time she was going back to Barons Reach, she had never asked her outright if she wanted to go with her again.

Grandma Mary had said something to her on their way home from Barons Reach that last morning though, that had stayed with her for years to come.

"Sometimes things change granddaughter, but it don't mean it the end."

Those words had sometimes returned to her thoughts over the years, but she couldn't see how they applied to her and Barons Reach, or even Jimba. Things had changed for her, but it *had* been the end! Perhaps for the first time ever, Grandma Mary had been wrong.

Therefore, she had felt confused for a time, by feeling guilty about not returning to Barons Reach.

However, she was finally able to accept her aunt and uncle's offer, when she decided she had probably only been worried that Aunt Grace might invite her to go to Barons Reach again, and she would be disappointed in her for not accepting her offer. But, it had been many years since her aunt had even mentioned Barons Reach to her, so there was no reason she would again, even if she were living with her.

At first, after moving into Dubbo with Aunt Grace and Uncle Dan, she spent most weekends back at Binda, as her mother and grandmother had hoped, and she often visited her grandmother at Jannali, the 4,000 acre wheat and sheep property next door. She found living in town, very different, and she missed the quietness of the bush, especially at night.

In town there always seemed to be some type of noise, either from a vehicle or a person's voice, carried by the wind. Occasionally though, she heard the familiar laugh of a kookaburra, which she always found soothing, for even though Dubbo was one of the biggest inland towns in New South Wales, it was still dotted with parks where several varieties of birds made their home. However, she mostly saw kookaburras in her favourite park by the riverbank, where she sometimes went to eat her lunch on workdays.

One of the Wiradjuri dreaming stories about the reason why a kookaburra laughs, comes to mind. She decides to recount it. Maybe it will help her fall asleep.

Long ago, the earth was in darkness, and the emu and the bush-turkey were always being mean to each other, throwing each other's eggs high into the sky. The moon and the stars were the campfires of all the sky people.

One day, the bush-turkey threw the emu's egg so high, it hit some wood from one of the campfires of the sky people and the spark that came from it created fire. The fire grew to light the whole earth, giving it warmth and colour, and became known as, the Sun.

After that, the sky people agreed to create the Sun every day, as long as they were reminded. So, they asked the kookaburra to laugh every morning to alert them.

When the kookaburra agreed, it became known as a brother, and from then on protected by the people below because of its important role.'

She remembers Grandma Mary telling her that the kookaburra – *gugubarra,* was her Wiradjuri totem too. Perhaps that why she enjoyed hearing their laughter so much. She felt close to them, and they always made her smile, and laugh also, when she heard them.

When her closest friend, Teagan, began her hairdressing apprenticeship at, Ahead of Hair, a popular hair salon in Dubbo, shortly after Libby had started to work at the Council, they would sometimes meet up at one of the parks in town to eat their lunch together.

The hair salon was just around the corner from the Council building, and only a block away from the main shopping area of Dubbo, so Teagan often coerced Libby into walking down the street to do some window-shopping after eating, before going back to work.

Libby preferred to go to the river. It was quieter there. However, her friend found it hard to sit still for long, and even harder to keep quiet, so she would often agree to walk down the street with her, to look-around. Libby decided she could always spend time at the river on her own, at other times.

They were in reality, very unlikely friends.

Libby was more often than not, a bit of an introvert, more than content to spend time in her own company, reading or being out of doors, walking in the bush. Teagan, on the other hand, was definitely an extrovert; always the life of any party and looking for distraction or excitement.

In several respects though, they complimented each other. Teagan helped Libby to become more sociable within the town community, and encouraged her to experience new things. Libby grounded Teagan, and helped her to realise that it was more important to have a few sincere friends than to have many who were superficial.

Their friendship began shortly after they both began High School. Students registered at Dubbo High School, from several primary schools in the town and district, but Libby naturally gravitated towards the faces she knew from Barwon Public School, and Teagan, to those she knew from Dubbo Public School.

Libby lived in the bush, had an older brother, and was from a close-knit family. Teagan lived in town, was an only child, and both her parents worked to provide a very comfortable life for their tiny family of three. However, they often worked late, and she rarely saw them.

In the first year of High School two distinct groups formed - the 'bushies' and the 'townies'.

Teagan quickly became the centre of attention of the townies, often coming to school with a different style of hair, wearing a new nail colour or lipstick. Everyone in this group gravitated towards Teagan. She always seemed to know what was in fashion and could even show them.

Meanwhile, the bushies generally remained leaderless. Most members of this group were content to keep their friendships on an equal par, as they had in primary school.

However, about a week into the first semester, a new girl arrived. Her name was Heather.

Heather wasn't particularly friendly from the onset, but it was obvious she was new to the district. Nobody knew her, or anything about her, except that she now lived in town. She sat by herself most of the time, except when a kind-hearted or lonely student attempted to get to know her. However, she quickly rebuffed any attempts of friendship and it became evident she wanted to be left alone.

However, one day she approached Teagan and her group, sitting under the trees around the sports oval, during lunch. Teagan was surprised at first, because she had already attempted to get to know Heather earlier in the week, without success.

Heather's personality and attitude seemed to have changed overnight. She was friendly, and she now seemed to want to get to know the townies. She told them she was from Sydney, and her family had moved to Dubbo to begin a new life in a rural area. She said she missed her friends in Sydney and was trying to get used to her new life. She listened attentively to the girl's as they described the things they did on the weekends, and the newest item of clothes or jewellery that they had recently bought. She showed great interest.

Teagan felt sorry for Heather. She could imagine how difficult it would be to leave all your friends and the place you had grown up in, behind. She decided she would try to include Heather in as many things as she could, to make her feel welcome.

Libby had noticed Heather attaching herself to the townies, and although she hadn't had much to do with Teagan, she had felt a little concerned for her.

She liked Teagan. She thought she was a bit overly concerned with her looks, but she was always nice to everyone. Libby knew her to be kind. However, she had a bad feeling about Heather.

She had approached Heather herself a few weeks back, when their History class had finished for the day. She had said hello and introduced herself, but Heather had just sneered at her, and walked off.

The encounter had reminded her of Roger.

A few weeks later during lunch, Libby was watching her brother mucking around with a football with some friends on the oval near the school auditorium, when she noticed Teagan and Heather by themselves, close by. She saw that sneer she remembered so well on Heather's face, and Teagan wearing a worried frown. Libby felt apprehensive.

She watched as Heather stretched out her arm and held her open palm towards Teagan, while Teagan moved her head from side-to-side. Teagan was clearly indicating, 'no', to what Heather was asking for.

The next minute Heather grabbed Teagan's arm and pulled her roughly. She then turned Teagan around to face forward, and held her tightly, with her arm. Heather then began reaching inside the top of Teagan's shirt with her other hand.

Libby didn't realise she was running towards the two girl's until she was nearly half-way from where she had been standing. She knew then that there was no turning back. She reached the girls, stood in front of Teagan, and looked behind her, straight into Heather's eyes.

"Let her go!" she said boldly.

Heather chuckled as she finally found the gold chain with the delicate pearl pendant around Teagan's neck that she had been looking for, and pulled it free of Teagan's shirt.

"Get lost bushie, mind your own business."

"I said, *let her go!*"

Heather gave the chain a hard jerk and it broke free. She pushed Teagan forward, into Libby. Libby held her ground, despite Teagan's body bumping into hers. Teagan found her balance and turned around to stand beside Libby.

Heather sneered at the two girls, and said, "There, I let her go. Now, piss off, both of you."

Libby didn't know what came over her. Instead of seeing Heather at that moment, she saw Roger walking away from the gate at Barons Reach, getting away with killing Tiger. She lunged towards Heather, pushing her to the ground. Teagan seemed to be in shock watching the event unfold.

Libby stood over Heather on the ground and said, "Give it back," as she held her hand out to the girl.

"You bitch," Heather growled, regaining her feet. She put the necklace in her left hand, glaring at Libby, and lifted her right arm with an open hand. Libby knew she was about to slap her, but she stood her ground and began to lift her arms to block it.

A hand suddenly grabbed Heather's outstretched wrist.

"I wouldn't do that if I were you."

Libby heard her brother's voice before she saw him, relief washing over her.

"Give it back to her," Will said, motioning to Teagan with his head.

Heather glared at Will, but she knew she was beaten. She belligerently threw the necklace at Teagan.

Will let go of her arm, but Heather began to look nervous. Just a few feet behind her, the wall of the auditorium loomed high and long, and Teagan, Libby and Will stood in a half circle, surrounding her.

"Don't ever mess with my sister or her friends, again. Ok?" Will said, gruffly. Then thinking he had done enough, he took a few steps back, allowing space for her to leave.

"Yeah, ok," Heather growled, and stormed off, looking tentatively over her shoulder every few steps until she was well away.

Libby and Teagan became close friends after that, and Heather never bothered either of them again.

Libby hugged her brother later when they were home, thanked him for helping her, and told him she had the best brother ever. He replied, with a sheepish grin, that he reckoned she probably would have sorted it herself, anyway, because even he had felt a bit intimidated by her fiery eyes and determined look.

The townies and the bushies groups became obsolete, due to Libby and Teagan's friendship. The girls from both groups began to mix more with each other, and while some paired off to become closer friends, overall they all remained friendly towards each other for the remainder of their High School years, and for many of them, in the years to come.

In the second year, after leaving High School, Libby moved from her aunt and uncle's home, into a unit with Teagan. They were both twenty years old when they signed the lease, in early 2004, a few months ago.

Her thoughts return to the photo she looked at earlier. Would Jimba still be at Barons Reach? But of course, Jimba was the same age as herself. He would probably be living and working somewhere else now, like she was. She is saddened by the thought, but doesn't really know why. She hadn't wanted to see him again after all, and she has no intention of returning to Barons Reach now, anyway.

What would he look like now though, at twenty? She had never really thought of him as aging at all; forever in her memory as the ten-year-old boy, she had once called her best friend. Would she even recognise him now, if she saw him? She tries to imagine him older, but only the image of his sandy hair, dark brown eyes and quick smile, that always made her feel happy, prevail.

She remembers how they used to sit in the big white gum tree, looking around at the countryside, exploring, creating adventures, swimming and splashing each other in the river. They had been so happy together then, had so much fun.

"I hope you're happy Jimba," she whispers wistfully, half asleep. "I'm sorry I didn't come back."

CHAPTER 6

Libby smiles as she drives slowly between the golden leaved poplar trees lining the front drive of Jannali. She loves visiting her grandparents, and she knows how lucky she is to have grown up living next door to them.

Today, she has driven from Dubbo to visit them for a special occasion, but whenever she thinks of her grandparents, she automatically thinks of the walking track that joins her home to theirs. She has been thinking about it, and other things, ever since she passed the Dubbo signpost on her way out of town.

The well-worn dirt track meanders between river gum trees, with trunks ranging from white-grey to red-brown, on both sides of the dividing fence between the two properties. As she strolled along, she would sometimes guess the colour of the trunk of the tree and its foliage that would appear around the next bend. She was often right, even with the change of the seasons.

Sometimes she would disturb a kangaroo grazing close by the track and it would bound away out of sight, camouflaged by the thick scrub between the trees. Yet, at other times, a kangaroo would only lift its head to glimpse at her as she passed, and return unperturbed to its meal.

She knew to make as much noise as she liked as she walked along in case there were snakes close by, especially the brown snakes in the summer time. However, they usually slithered away if they heard noise, especially when Tiger had been around.

She would often come across Sulphur Crested cockatoos perched in the trees above her. The cockatoos were hard not to notice with their brilliant white plumage and bright yellow crests, against the greenery of the trees. Sometimes they would fly away screeching as if in mortal danger.

In contrast, the black and white magpies would often stare at her, scrutinizing her face for recognition. Then, confident she looked familiar and posed no threat, they would warble in greeting.

When the kookaburras laughed, she laughed with them, and silently thanked them for their welcome.

She thinks about the dreaming story that explains how the birds got their colour from the first rainbow arch in the sky:

'At first the arch was only fairly small, but as it began to suck in more and more red, blue, green, yellow and purple colours from all around, it started to grow and pulsate.

Eventually, it grew so big - it exploded! The rainbow became a million pieces that floated in the air as they slowly drifted toward the ground. And, as the million colourful pieces fell towards the ground, the pieces then changed into all the birds we know today.

Some of the birds, like the crow, didn't like the feeling of falling, and they screamed out in horror, making the sound: Aaahh, Aaahh. Other birds, like the kookaburra, thought it was the funniest feeling they had ever had and started to laugh, making the sound: Haahaaa, Haahaaa. And still, other birds thought it was the most wonderful feeling of all, so they spread their wings wide, opened their throats, and started to sing the most beautiful songs you could ever hear.

And that's how the birds got their colours and their voices — because of that rainbow, way back in the Dreamtime.

When Libby and her brother, Will, were younger, Grandma Mary would usually accompany them as they walked back to Binda from a visit at Jannali. At those times, she would always stop at the river on the Binda side of the big old gum tree, the halfway point of the track between the two properties. It was easy to see that the river was important to her grandmother. After they passed the big old gum tree, she would give them both a quick hug before they continued on the track to their home. However, every time Libby had looked back at her grandmother, she had noticed her walk over to the old log near the riverbank, and sit and stare into the water.

One day Libby raced back to the log where her grandmother was sitting, and sat quietly beside her. Grandma Mary had turned to her and said "The river tell you things granddaughter. You just have to listen carefully." Then she told Libby to go and catch up to Will.

Grandma Mary has taught them lots of things about the Wiradjuri ways, and Libby knows more than Will because she has spent more time with her grandmother, not only at Jannali but also at Barons Reach.

Their mother often recited the dreaming stories to them both when they were very little, so Will has heard them too. However, Libby has heard her grandmother tell them so many times at Barons Reach at the story-telling, she can recall them now, word-for-word, at any time.

Grandma Mary told Libby and Will that she taught their father the ways of the Wiradjuri when he was very young. She said he then taught their mother when they became friends. Grandma Mary then taught Aunt Grace, when she came to live at Jannali, and now Aunt Grace is teaching anyone who comes to visit Barons Reach. She told Libby and Will that it would be up to them to teach their children one day.

"That the way to keep the Wiradjuri way from gettin' lost," she said, looking intently into their eyes.

She told them that the Wiradjuri people once looked after a very big part of New South Wales, from the Blue Mountains in the east, to the town of Hay in the west, north to the town of Nyngan, and south to the town of Albury.

Libby had been to the Blue Mountains on the way to Sydney, and passed the turn off to Nyngan on a family trip to the Warrumbungle National Park near Coonabarabran, so she had a pretty good idea of how big the area was that her grandmother was talking about.

Grandma Mary said that that area was once known as 'the land of the three rivers', by the Wiradjuri people. But, she added, that was when the Macquarie River was called - the Wambool, the Lachlan River was called - the Kalare, and the Murrumbidgee River was called - the Murrumbidjeri.

Another time, she had shown them the carving in the big old gum tree by the river. She said she knew it had been carved by a Wiradjuri person, not only because the tree was in Wiradjuri country, but because she recognised the circular, diamond and spiral shaped designs, cut deeply within. She said each tribe had their own special markings.

Grandma Mary told Libby and Will that their parents had brought the track back to life again. She said that was when their father lived with her and Grandpa Don at Jannali, and their mother lived with her mother and father at Binda. The two children had often met at the river near that big old white gum tree when they were little.

Libby had been a little confused at the time though and asked, "Well, how come Nana and Pop didn't stay at Binda, where Mum grew up? I mean, you still live here Grandma Mary, where Dad grew up?"

Grandma Mary then explained that her Nana and Pop had passed the land on back to them, or as they would say, they *sold* Binda to them, because they had to move into town. So, after her father and mother grew up and were married, they moved into the house at Binda, to start their own family.

That was why her father looks after the land at Binda and Grandpa Don looks after the land at Jannali. She said that at one time, Grandpa Don's family had looked after a great deal more land that people now live on in the Dubbo area, including Binda. But, she added, that was before Grandpa Don's grandfather needed money to clear his debts.

She said it didn't matter though, that Grandpa's grandfather had done that, because Grandpa Don and her father still had more than enough land to look after, and even enough for her brother Will to take care of when he was old enough.

Libby knew by then that Grandma Mary held a different view than most people about the ownership of land. According to her grandmother, no one ever really *owned* land.

She told Libby that her Wiradjuri mother and grandmother taught her lots of things, but the most important thing of all was to remember that we are only the *caretakers* of the land, and if we look after it, it will look after us. She said that that was the Wiradjuri way of things, but there were also white people who respected the land too, like Grandpa Don.

She also told Libby that the Wiradjuri people had been caretakers of the land they now live on for a very, very long time, before the first white person ever set foot in the area. And, that first white person was Grandpa Don's great grandfather, Samuel Rutherford, She said she knew he had respected the Wiradjuri people, because he had written in a diary about how he had fired some men he had working for him for being unkind to the aborigines.

He also described how the Wiradjuri people even helped him to build his house by showing him what natural materials he should use from the area. That house was the very same house that Grandma Mary and Grandpa Don now lived in. As it was so old and special, it was even Heritage Listed, and Libby knew all about what that entailed, now that she worked at the Dubbo Council.

The front drive ends, and she is at the homestead. She parks the Mazda beside the Holden Commodore belonging to her aunt and switches off the engine. Uncle Dan's 4-wheel-drive, her mother's station wagon and her father's ute are also parked nearby, so it looks like all her family have arrived.

Aunt Grace and her mother are cooking the family dinner tonight, so they would have been here first.

Uncle Dan probably only arrived a little before Libby, along with her father and brother after they had all finished work for the day. Will had most likely come with their father.

Her mother, father and brother all still used the walking track, but it was quicker to drive from one house to the other. It took less than five minutes. They rarely used the walking track at night anyway.

She looks fondly at the house in the fading light. Some people would say it just looked like an old run-down house. They would be right about it being old, but not run-down.

It was the very first house built in the area by a white person, her great-great-great grandfather. She had had to work out how many *greats* to add, with her grandmother's help.

The house was an original slab-hut, made from timber, bark, mud, clay, and other natural materials, and these days that made it of great historical significance.

Not far from the house, the original sandstone stables complex also still stands, though commonly referred to by everyone in the family as – the shed. It originally consisted of a blacksmith's forge, coach room, sunken cool room, storeroom and stable, although Grandpa Don's father had it altered slightly to include a more modern shearing shed.

The interior of the house could probably be best described as – enchanting. It had been updated to accommodate more-modern conveniences, but retained a semblance of old-fashioned charm with an imposing sitting room, tent-shaped plaster ceiling and 1950's patterned wallpaper.

Her grandparents still used some original furnishings, including an iron bed and campaign chest in the master bedroom.

When she thinks about it, the houses at Barons Reach and Jannali couldn't be more different, even though they were both built around the same time.

The house at Barons Reach was big and grand, while the Jannali house countered that by being cosy and unimposing. Yet, both houses seemed to exude a sense of authority in their structures. It was as if they both knew their special importance.

Both houses were Heritage Listed, built by the first white men in the areas of Dubbo and Bathurst; Wiradjuri country.

Grandma Mary and Aunt Grace both told Libby that their ancestors, who built these houses, had not intentionally harmed the Wiradjuri people, even if they had still attributed to it by arriving in the area. Libby was proud to know that, at least.

Of course, she knew it had been very hard for all Indigenous Australians after the white men came.

Applying what Grandma Mary, Aunt Grace and her mother had told her, to what she had been taught at school, read and heard on the news, she knew a great deal more than most Australians about the effect white man had on Australia's first people. Well, more than white Australians, at any rate. Knowing about something was nowhere near the same as actually going through the experience, as the aboriginals and their descendants had.

When she was a teenager, Libby's mother told her about Grandma Mary's early life as one of the stolen generation, and how Aunt Grace had been taken away for adoption, because she was the child of a part aboriginal mother and a white father. She had then better understood what drove Aunt Grace and Grandma Mary to do what they did at Barons Reach.

She had realised then how fortunate she was to have been born with white man's blood. She did not look at all aboriginal either. In fact, none of her family who had aboriginal blood did, except her grandmother, who could only be slightly recognised as having aboriginal blood by her honey coloured skin.

Yet, all her family were proud of their aboriginal ancestry, or that they had married a part aboriginal, as was the case for her mother, uncle and grandfather. And, the person responsible for instilling that pride and ensuring that no one in her family ever forgot about the Wiradjuri ways, was Grandma Mary, the daughter of a full-blooded Wiradjuri woman.

It had taken a very long time for the Australia government to begin to recognise and admit to the impact white man had, and was still having, on Indigenous Australians, but at least there was – progress.

In 1993, when Libby was nine years old, she watched Prime Minister Paul Keating, on television, give a speech in which he stated:

'It begins, I think, with the act of recognition. Recognition, that it was *we* who did the dispossessing. *We* took the traditional lands and smashed the traditional way of life. *We* brought the disasters, the alcohol. *We* committed the murders. *We* took the children from their mothers. *We* practised discrimination and exclusion.'

Yes, however slow, there was still - progress…

Libby picks up her handbag and the little parcel wrapped in pink rose designed paper, from the front passenger seat beside her, and quickly alights from her car.

She hopes her grandmother likes the hanging crystal ball she has bought for her for her 70th birthday. She will suggest she hang it from the curtain rail in the kitchen. That way, it will catch the morning sun and send slivers of pretty coloured-lights around the room. She smiles at the thought of her grandmother enjoying it each morning.

She walks over to the front door of the homestead, opens it, and half-sings, "Hallo, it's meee," as she enters.

She can hear voices coming from the lounge room, and concludes she hasn't been heard. She closes the front door behind her and continues along the hallway to the lounge room.

She has been smiling in anticipation of seeing her grandmother, but her smile disappears the moment she enters the room.

Her grandmother is sitting in one of the plush lounge chairs with one leg outstretched on a footstool, a look of pain etched on her face.

Aunt Grace is speaking to her, "Mum, I think we need to take you into town to the hospital to get it checked."

Grandma Mary notices Libby at the door. "Hallo granddaughter," she says, making a brave effort to smile at her.

Aunt Grace and Libby's mother turn towards the door and smile briefly at Libby, acknowledging her presence.

Grandpa Don, in the matching single lounge chair beside his wife, and Libby's father, brother and uncle, standing close by, glance her way, but immediately return concerned looks towards Mary.

"Oh Grandma," Libby exclaims, racing over and kneeling beside the chair, dropping her handbag and gift on the floor nearby. Reaching for her grandmother's hand on the armrest, she asks, "What happened?"

"It ok granddaughter, don't you worry. I just not lookin' where I goin'. Just tripped," she says, as she begins to pat her granddaughter's arm in reassurance with her other hand.

Libby can see her grandmother is trying to be brave and it hurts to see her in pain. She looks up at her mother and notices she is looking at her aunt. It looks like they are sharing a silent conversation.

Her grandmother follows her eyes and it seems she has heard their silent conversation. "Now, there no point you tryin' to get me to leave my home on my birthday when all me family 'round me, to sit in that hospital waitin' room all night, and then when I finally get to see a doctor, he just tell me to rest it."

The women instantly look towards Libby's grandfather, for support.

"Well, you should know by now, there's no way she'll do anything she doesn't want to," he says resignedly, looking at Mary with exasperation and shaking his head from side-to-side.

Satisfied, now that Don has backed her up, Mary adds, "So, let's get this party back on track, hey?"

So, despite everyone's concern, the family all rallied to lighten the mood for Mary's sake.

Libby's father and uncle moved the lounge chair Mary had been sitting on into the dining room, arranging it so she could sit comfortably at the head of the table, sideways, with her leg elevated on a footstool.

Dinner was served, a tray arranged for Mary, and despite an occasional grimace, the delight on her face made it clear she was enjoying herself as much as possible.

Her face even beamed when she looked around at her family singing 'happy birthday', after she blew the candles out that were arranged in the number – 70, on her cake.

Libby was thrilled when her grandmother exclaimed with delight at the hanging crystal ball. But when Libby made the suggestion about hanging it from the curtain rail in the kitchen, she said, "I might do that later granddaughter, but for now I want it close by, so I can hold it up to the light where ever I am."

***

The next day, while at the river during her lunch hour at work, Libby called her mother to ask how her grandmother was. She knew she would be keeping a watchful eye on her after her fall the previous night.

Her mother said that she had checked up on her that morning. Her entire knee was badly bruised and she was having difficulty walking, so she insisted she let her take her to the doctor. She had called the Medical Centre and booked an appointment that morning, after Mary relented. Mary said she agreed only because although there was usually a long wait at the Medical Centre, even with an appointment, it was still far better than having to wait much longer at the hospital. However, the doctor took one look at Mary's leg and straight away ordered an x-ray, so Mary had had to go to the hospital anyway. When the results came back, the doctor said she had been very lucky, especially for a woman her age. There were no broken bones, so the doctor prescribed some medication for inflammation and advised Mary to rest her leg.

Libby's mother had chuckled when telling Libby, "Of course, you can imagine what your grandmother said to that…*See, I told yous. He just tellin' me to rest it*," she fondly mimicked Libby's grandmother.

Libby was relieved to hear the news and she knew that her mother and Aunt Grace would be constant visitors at Jannali, even more than they normally were, while her grandmother recuperated.

It was good that Aunt Grace didn't have to work, although she was still always very busy with community projects and fund-raising in Dubbo, as well as doing the tours at Barons Reach.

A recent conversation she overheard, between her mother and aunt, comes to mind.

Her mother had said she was beginning to think the trips to Barons Reach were getting to be too much for Mary. However, she had added, even if someone were to drive her there and back to save her the long drive, it would still be near to impossible to persuade her to give up the story-telling.

Her aunt had then replied that she had been thinking the same thing, about all the driving. She said she had been considering coming back to Jannali and picking Mary up, then doubling back to Dubbo and on to Bathurst. The only drawback though, she added, would be that Mary would sometimes need to stay longer than she normally would, because sometimes Aunt Grace had to stay longer to attend to other things.

As for the story-telling, her aunt agreed, and even if she could be persuaded to give it up, she would insist upon finding a Wiradjuri person to replace her. Aunt Grace said that might prove difficult. So, she said, she had decided that when the time came that Mary could definitely no longer continue, she would just need to do the story-telling herself. She said she knew she wouldn't be as good as Mary, but at least Mary would have some comfort knowing there was still a descendant of the Wiradjuri family doing it.

Libby stares into the river, mesmerized by the water. "The river tell you things granddaughter. You just have to listen carefully," her grandmother once said…

Was she now hearing a message from Barons Reach?

CHAPTER 7

Libby glances at her grandmother in the passenger seat beside her as she navigates the winding road ahead. Grandma Mary's eyes are closed, but Libby is certain she is still awake. Every time they pass a landmark, her eyes open, and after a quick perusal of the scene ahead, they close again.

Although she had only been ten-years-old and a passenger when she had last travelled this road, she has no trouble remembering it. Besides, it was pretty much - straight forward, signposted all the way.

They were on the last stretch of the journey. They had just passed an old building after crossing the bridge. The building had once been a general store, evident from the faded sign on the cracked window. Libby remembered it, although understandably, it had looked a lot older this time.

Once again, her grandmother had opened her eyes as they approached the bridge, and closed them shortly after they had passed the old building. Libby is now certain her grandmother could navigate this journey blindfolded.

She reaches the top of a small hill and takes an inward breath as she looks across, past her grandmother. And there it is - Murruway! She's surprised she's remembered the name of the homestead. She isn't able to recall anyone mentioning the new name since she first heard it spoken by Grandma Mary, all those years ago.

As if on cue, her grandmother opens her eyes. This time they stay open.

"Here we are!" she announces, as Libby descends the hill and manoeuvres the car towards the front gates of Barons Reach.

She ponders the possibility that her grandmother can see through her eyelids. In any event, although she always enjoys her company, she is glad she dozed almost the entire journey.

The quietness had allowed her to think freely, with nothing to interrupt her thoughts as she automatically followed the road and sign posts, and admired the beauty of the countryside they passed. She had forgotten how pretty the countryside was around Bathurst.

It would have seemed natural if she had been remembering her last unhappy day at Barons Reach, but instead, her thoughts had roamed to earlier, carefree days - with Jimba. She wouldn't have been able to conceal the smiles that had lit up her face at the memories, so she had been relieved by her grandmother's closed eyelids.

She had therefore not needed to disclose her private thoughts. Even though they were good memories, she didn't want to share them with anyone. No, she wanted to savour and play with them, hold them close to her heart - protect them, so no one could ever tarnish or take their sweetness away; those happiest days of her life.

She had made the offer to be her grandmother's driver for visits to Barons Reach, the previous weekend at a family card-game night, organised by her mother and aunt, to lift her grandmother's spirits after her recent fall.

They all knew how to play 500 and Canasta. Libby's mother had taught Libby and Will when they were young, and their father had sometimes joined in as a fourth person, so they could play as pairs. Grandpa Don had taught Grandma Mary, Aunt Grace, Libby and Will's father, and Uncle Dan had picked it up from watching them all.

After her last visit to the river in town, a few days prior, Libby knew she held the solution to her grandmother's current dilemma. She had recently overheard her aunt telling her mother that the visitor tours at Barons Reach were now limited to the weekends, so there was nothing preventing her from taking her grandmother to them now; it wouldn't interfere with her Monday to Friday work.

Her mother was always busy looking after her father and brother, and keeping an eye on Grandpa Don when Grandma Mary was away, so it wasn't really possible for her to step in. And, as far as she knew, Aunt Grace still sometimes stayed longer than Grandma Mary at Barons Reach after the tours, so they still needed two vehicles.

She imagined her grandmother would accept her offer, though be a little disheartened because it would remind her of her current lack of independence. She also imagined that her aunt would show a small measure of relief.

However, the responses to her proposal by every member of her family, completely took her by surprise.

Aunt Grace sighed so deeply, Libby almost wondered if she had lost her breath, and she almost lost her own when her aunt then spontaneously pulled her into the biggest of bear hugs.

Her mother smiled so approvingly Libby almost felt embarrassed.

Grandpa Don's eyes glistened with tears as he said, 'Thank you Libby dear."

It was apparent her offer also gained immense approval from her father, when his chest puffed up with pride and he immediately said, "Good girl," while nodding his head to support his praise.

Uncle Dan rushed over, put his arm around her shoulder and pecked her on the cheek, and even her brother, Will, added, "Good on ya sis," and patted her on the back as though she were the recipient of an award.

Completely thrown by the ardent responses from those family members, she then remained speechless by her grandmother's.

Mary beamed so much with joy that if Libby hadn't known better she would have been convinced her grandmother had injured herself deliberately, just so she would go back to Barons Reach with her. But then, her grandmother's words almost brought tears to her eyes, and she admonished herself for even entertaining the idea.

"You a real good granddaughter Libby. Yep! No one ever have a granddaughter as good as you."

However, even though her grandmother's words had been well intended, and her family's words and actions had all been overwhelmingly, heart-warming, Libby felt so undeserving of it all.

Had she really been so blind? Did her grandmother really need to have hurt herself, before she had taken any notice? Their reactions had opened her eyes to the fact that she had been the only one who had not seen the need for her to help her grandmother and aunt in this way

- long before now. She had held her driver's licence for several years now. She could have been helping a lot earlier. Had she been so self-centered that she had failed to see what she now believed her family had already hoped for all along? Now that she could see how much it meant, especially to her grandmother, she concluded: *she hadn't been good to her grandmother – she hadn't been a good granddaughter.*

Were the memories of Roger, Tiger and Jimba *so* bad that she had put them before her family's needs? Perhaps when she had been a child, it had been understandable. Even now, she finds it difficult to imagine she could ever forgive Roger, no matter how mixed up he may have been. But - she had allowed her hate towards him to blind her. If she hadn't been so focussed upon keeping hate at bay, she would have clearly been able to see where love was needed, instead.

As for Jimba, well she had truly shown him how displeased she had been with him. After all, she had given him the cold shoulder for *ten* years. Yet, he had only been a child when she had instigated her punishment. The impact of now realising the extent of her unkindness to him almost makes her cry. Of course she could be civil to him now. How could she have been so horrible? She could have, *should* have, returned to Barons Reach, told him how hurt she had felt, and – forgiven him. Isn't that what she would have asked of him?

But, it was too late now. She would probably never see him again, she reminded herself. She would just have to accept that she had wronged him, and hope that he has somehow been able to forgive her for being so unkind all those years ago. She then understood why she had felt sad when thinking about him recently, not to mention – guilty, when thinking of Barons Reach.

She put those thoughts aside though, to concentrate on her grandmother instead. She was the main reason she was going back now anyway. Although it had been close to three weeks since her fall, she was still hobbling around, and much to her annoyance, she needed help with even every-day things.

Aunt Grace had insisted Grandma Mary go back to the doctors for a check-up before agreeing to let Libby drive her to Barons Reach. Grandma Mary had still argued about it, of course.

"There's no need to see the doctor. Even though it my drivin' leg, I still not drivin', cause my granddaughter drivin'," she had said in exasperation.

Aunt Grace had then very gently asked her if she would see the doctor for *her* sake, because otherwise she would be worrying about her the whole time they were at Barons Reach.

She had eventually complied, though somewhat grudgingly, and when the doctor said her leg was slowly improving, she looked at Grace with that well-known look which always meant, "See, I told ya!"

When Libby told Teagan about Barons Reach, she was astounded. She was also indignant.

"Elisabeth Rutherford, why haven't you told me about this before?" she declared, looking at her with complete annoyance.

"Well, I haven't been back for over ten years and we have only known each other since High School," she said in her defence.

"I guess," Teagan responded, still looking at her as if she really didn't know her. "But, I've mentioned your aunt before. Like when she has been in the paper with all the things she's involved in. I mean, *everyone* knows who she is in Dubbo. You could have told me about this property she owns near Bathurst."

"Oh Teagan, why would you have been interested in that?"

Teagan had then pouted, and Libby couldn't hold back a little chuckle.

"You hairdressers just have to know every *thing* about every *one* in this town. Don't you?"

Teagan had then given up feigning offence, and also chuckling, said, "Yeah, I guess. But I can't help it if everyone wants to talk when I do their hair."

Libby didn't tell Teagan about Jimba, or Tiger and Roger. She only told her about the tours, and that she would be assisting her grandmother at Barons Reach, as well as driving her there and back home.

Aunt Grace told her that although they now only did weekend tours, they still had one at least every three weeks, although they had three coming up in a row, in the following three weeks.

With the disclosure of Barons Reach and the tours, Teagan now became aware that Libby was part Wiradjuri. Although Libby didn't doubt for a second that it would affect their friendship, she hadn't been at all prepared for her reaction.

"Oh Libby, now I know why you are so glamourous, and why your aunt and grandmother are so good looking. I knew your grandmother had something else. I always thought she must have been Asian, because of her skin colour. I had no idea it was aboriginal. Wow,

I bet you have some stories you could tell me about that side of the family."

Libby knew Teagan spoke out of interest and that if she were to tell her about the injustices her grandmother and aunt had experienced, she would have nothing but sorrow and sympathy for them. But, those stories were only for her grandmother and aunt to tell, if they chose to.

She could however, tell Teagan about the Wiradjuri culture, and that was something she took pride in doing. Teagan listened attentively, especially to the dreaming stories, and Libby felt that her grandmother would be proud of her in the way she told them; just like she did.

***

Libby sits beside Grandma Mary at the fire. So far, her grandmother has complied with Aunt Grace's request to take it easy. She has only walked when it has been necessary, and she has been resting for most of the day.

Libby had stayed downstairs with her earlier that afternoon, while Aunt Grace took the tour of the upstairs of the house, and they had even stayed at the house during Aunt Grace's reading at the gravesite.

However, by the time they had all finished tea, Grandma Mary still looked tired, despite her rest. Yet, she insisted she would be fine for the story-telling, so Libby drove her to the fire-site, and has remained by her side, ever since.

Libby has really noticed the different in her grandmother tonight though, despite her obvious enjoyment of being at Barons Reach and meeting new people interested in the Wiradjuri ways.

She seemed to be her usual self while reciting the stories or talking to people, but the moment she stopped, she'd lean back into her chair and stare vacantly into the fire, until someone interrupted her.

Libby has always remembered her looking around eagerly, scrutinizing faces for recognition and half jumping out of her seat to speak to someone who walked over to her to talk. But, that was when she had been a lot younger, she reminds herself.

She has just finished the dreaming story about the kookaburra and as she had earlier, she now leans back in her camp chair. This time, however, she sighs deeply.

"Are you alright Grandma," Libby asks, a frown of worry creasing her forehead. She hopes she is not in any pain.

"Yes, granddaughter. I just feelin' a bit tired. But I wonderin'...," she says, pausing, looking into her granddaughter's eyes, "...would you tell the last story for the night? You know, the one about the kangaroo?"

Libby is momentarily tongue-tied. She isn't sure if she is confident enough to do it, but her grandmother is looking at her, almost pleadingly. Why not, she decides. I still remember all the dreaming stories, and she had recently had some practice reciting them to Teagan.

So when the crowd quietened again, Mary announced that her granddaughter would tell the last dreaming story for the night. She then made herself more comfortable in her chair and closed her eyes.

Libby began the dreaming story of, 'how the kangaroo got her pouch', a little hesitantly at first. However, when she saw the eager looks on the faces of the visitors, listening so intently, her words began to flow much more confidently.

Towards the end of the story, now relaxed, she began looking more closely at the crowd. She noticed a man standing right at the back, on the other side of the fire, his face in shadow. She almost paused in telling the story, because somehow she felt drawn to focus on him. He stood completely still, and she couldn't see anything but his shadowed outline. But then, as if reading her thoughts, he moved out of the shadow and his face was suddenly exposed.

At that moment, her story ended, and as she scrutinized the man's face, she saw he was looking directly back into hers. He then smiled, and she knew without doubt - it was Jimba.

***

"Hello Libby," he says, standing beside her, as she remains seated in the camp chair. "Or, should I be calling you Elizabeth now?"

"No, no. Still Libby - most of the time," she replies, trying hard not to stare at him as she stands.

He's so tall now, and – *handsome!* Though he'd been a good-looking boy, she could never have imagined he would end up looking this good.

"So, you're still here Jimba?"

"He go by Jim now granddaughter," her grandmother interrupts, with her eyes still closed.

"Oh, sorry," Libby says, not moving her eyes from Jimba's.

She's thankful it's night, because she's sure her face would now be red with embarrassment.

"No problem," he replies, a gentle upturn of his lips, an indication of slight amusement, "but *you* can call me anything you like Libby," he adds, now looking serious and staring intently into her eyes.

She suddenly feels uncomfortable, and because her grandmother has acutely reminded her of her presence, she decides it would be best to get her back to the house.

Jim seems to recognise her unrest. "Well, I won't keep you. I expect you'll be wanting to go ho… back to the house."

He remains looking at Libby, as he adds, "Night, Mrs Rutherford."

Mary opens her eyes, and responds gruffly, "Now how many times I got to tell you Jim, it Mary to you. I know you nearly all ya life." A twinkle in her eye now indicates she had not been serious with her gruffness.

Jim chuckles. "Ok - Mary."

"That better. Now granddaughter, time for us to go," she says, and Libby helps her grandmother out of the camp chair.

"See you around, Libby?" Jim half states, half asks, and without waiting for a reply, walks briskly away.

***

Libby wanted to question her grandmother about Jimba, or Jim, as she must now train herself to call him. However, it would have to wait, because during the short drive back to the house she had been trying to absorb the fact that she had seen him again, to voice any questions.

Aunt Grace was in the office, working on paperwork, when they arrived back at the house. She came out to see if either of them needed anything, but Libby and her grandmother assured her they were fine, so she bade them goodnight and quickly returned to the office.

After ensuring her grandmother was settled for the night, she considered going to the office and asking her aunt about Jim, but she remembered how busy she had seemed earlier, so she decided to retire to bed instead.

What would be the point in talking to her aunt about him anyway? Jim was obviously either still living at Barons Reach, or he came to help with the tours, such as preparing the fire for the story-telling, like he used to with his father. Her grandmother had spoken to him earlier as if she had seen him often enough, so it looked like he was at least usually here for the tours.

Well, she could confirm that with either her grandmother or aunt, tomorrow. There would be nothing wrong with that. After all, they had once been friends. She was just interested.

Perhaps she wouldn't need to ask her grandmother or aunt though.

Before Libby had left the recent family card game night, along with telling her there were visitor tours lined up for the following three weeks in a row, Aunt Grace had also told her that the first of the tours coming up would be different from the others.

She said that although the visitor tours now only consisted of one full afternoon and evening, on a Saturday, that wouldn't be the case for the following weekend, Libby's first visit back to Barons Reach.

On a usual weekend tour, they would arrive on the Friday evening and leave on the Sunday morning, except for Aunt Grace who sometimes stayed longer. However, Aunt Grace had made bookings on the Sunday as well this time, which had been made before Grandma Mary had injured herself. That meant that although she and Grandma Mary would still arrive on Friday evening, they wouldn't be able to leave for Dubbo and Jannali until Monday morning.

Aunt Grace had apologised profusely to Libby about the Sunday booking. She knew that Libby hadn't expected she would need to take time off work when she had made her offer to drive her grandmother to Barons Reach for tours.

Libby had reassured her that she was sure it wouldn't be a problem, and she had confirmed it after her application for leave was approved at work, for the following Monday. Aunt Grace said that from now on she would definitely limit the tours to Saturdays only.

Therefore, as they needed to stay for the extra day this time, she just might have the opportunity to see Jim before she left. Perhaps what had seemed like an inconvenience had suddenly turned around to her advantage.

Lying in bed, she thinks about their plans they had organised earlier that evening, for tomorrow.

Aunt Grace had begun organising some downstairs cupboards earlier that morning, but it had turned into a bigger job than she had originally thought. She still hadn't completed it by lunchtime. Then, straight after lunch, she had had the upstairs tour. She said she didn't like leaving a job half done though, so she hoped she would have time to finish the remaining cupboards tomorrow, before the upstairs house tour and gravesite reading in the afternoon. She said she would probably have been able to finish the cupboards by the time the story-telling would be over tonight, but she needed to finish some bookwork instead, in readiness for an appointment with her accountant in Bathurst on Monday morning.

Aunt Grace also said she would now need to be back in Dubbo by Monday afternoon, instead of Tuesday, as originally intended. That was because just as she had been about to leave Dubbo on Friday, she had received a call from a charity organiser in Dubbo, inviting her to a fundraising morning-tea on Tuesday.

Libby was always amazed at how her aunt managed to juggle things between Dubbo and Bathurst.

After listening to Aunt Grace's itinerary for the next few days, Libby had felt sorry for her and immediately offered to do the upstairs tour of the house tomorrow. That was, she said, if Aunt Grace thought she would be able to do it, and as long as Grandma Mary didn't mind being left on her own. That way, her aunt would have a bit more time, if she needed it, to finish organising the cupboards the next day.

Grandma Mary assured Libby she would be just fine on her own, and it was evident by her aunt's kind smile and words, that her offer was appreciated.

"Thank you Libby dear," she said, readily accepting her offer. "That will be wonderful. I'm so glad you're here. And, yes, of course you'll be able to do it. I'll give you the brochures, which have all the historical details of the house and the particular rooms they'll follow you to. All you really need to do is lead the visitors upstairs and to each room in turn. If you like, you can also read the information out to them as you go. There's no need to have it memorised like I have. I have just been doing it for so many years that I now know it by heart."

Libby had been very relieved by her aunt's reassurance. She probably wouldn't have offered, if she had thought more about it first. She wasn't usually comfortable with being the centre of attention. Nonetheless, it seemed her grandmother had also decided she was quite capable too, asking her to help with the story-telling, as she had this evening. Well, she had come back to Barons Reach to help out, so she may as well take every opportunity to do so, in any way she can.

So, she would be doing the upstairs tour after lunch, and then she would drive her grandmother to the gravesite reading, or stay with her at the house if she didn't feel up to it. It would then be time for tea, before going to the story-telling.

She will most likely see Jim at the story-telling again, although her grandmother will be close by. Of course, that wouldn't normally matter, but she would just rather have the opportunity to speak with him in private.

Therefore, she decides, in order to speak to Jim alone, she will need to find him after breakfast. That will be the only opportunity she will have this visit, and as it will be a Sunday, there will be more chance he will be at home too.

To think, she hadn't wanted to see him for ten years, and now she is searching for every opportunity. But, it wasn't only because she wanted to apologise to him for not returning. She must admit, she now finds herself very attracted to him, in a way she has never felt towards any male before. She finds this thought is a little unsettling, but she decides it is most likely only because she wants to feel good about him again, so she is probably only imagining it. She would just need to get used to the now grown-up Jim, and then she probably wouldn't feel that attraction anymore, she reassures herself.

When she stood up after he had appeared beside her, she had noticed how tall he was. He had to be over six foot. She could tell because she knew her brother was six foot, exactly, and Jim had towered over her five foot, nine inches, a little more than her brother.

She can't help but smile when she remembers how she was always put out that he was taller than her when they were little. Well, she doesn't mind at all now.

Again, comparing him physically to her brother, because Will was very fit from working on the land, Jim has even wider shoulders and a stronger build too, although two years younger. So, whatever Jim had been doing the last ten years had obviously kept him fit and in very good shape.

However, his smile was the same, and it was his smile, which had given him away tonight; the way his entire face lit up, his eyes sparkled, the dimples in both cheeks deepened. It had always made her happy just to see him smile. That was something she had never been able to forget, and the image of it stays in her mind as she drifts off to sleep.

CHAPTER 8

Libby closes the garden gate behind her, and begins striding purposefully along the trail to the workmen's section of the property.

With breakfast over, Grandma Mary had decided to relax on the verandah, and Aunt Grace had said she would join her for a little while, before getting back to organising the cupboards.

When Libby said she might go for a walk, they both said that was a great idea, almost in unison. It seemed they couldn't get rid of her fast enough. Perhaps they wanted to talk in private; have a mother – daughter discussion. Libby didn't mind in the least. She had something she had to do.

She arrives at the first house in the workmen's area, and automatically walks up to the house she remembers as Jim's. It was still a nice looking house. It had always been well kept, even though there hadn't been much of a garden. It had been obvious that no woman had lived there. The lawn had always been neatly edged, but the only sign of any floral addition had been some wild looking geraniums along the interior of the front house-yard.

There were about half a dozen workmen's houses on Barons Reach, all spaced apart enough to ensure some privacy for the occupants. Only two of the houses had been family homes though, and the Manager's home stood out as the biggest and nicest of all.

Jim lived alone with his father, Luke Ferguson, in one of the family houses. Luke applied for the - live onsite Farm Hand position, at Barons Reach, shortly after Grace arrived as the new owner. The Property Manager, Bill Sutton, and Grace, gave him an interview. He had the necessary experience and references required for the position. He said there was just one thing he needed to let them know though, while they considered his application.

He had a five-year-old son, named Jimba. He told them that Jimba's mother had only recently died from a terminal disease, and he was all the family he had. He could only work for them if he could bring his son with him to live at Barons Reach. Jimba was old enough to start Kindergarten, so he could put him on the school bus, which he had already found out drove past the front gates of Barons Reach every school day.

Bill, and his daughter, had lived at Barons Reach for many years. He saw no problem with granting Luke's request. His daughter was attending the local TAFE, 'technical and further education' institute, in Bathurst, catching the same school bus as the regular primary and secondary school students. He could ask her to keep an eye on the young fella. She was studying, 'Childcare' too, so she had a fondness for younger children. She might even look out for Jimba in the afternoons after school, while Luke was still working.

Grace had been greatly relieved by Bill's ready acceptance of Luke's son. She had felt overwhelming compassion for the man's situation, and she had been prepared to debate fervently with Bill if he had not shown his assent, especially when he had a daughter living at Barons Reach too. However, she was acutely aware she was responsible for ensuring all decisions made were for the good of Barons Reach, and its occupants, so she would still have seriously considered Bill's thoughts on the matter, even if he had not agreed with her. That it had been a mutual agreement to hire Luke Ferguson though, had strengthened Grace and Bill's relationship.

During the first few years, Luke and Jimba lived at Barons Reach, the Property Managers daughter had in fact kept an eye on Jimba. She had become almost like a big sister to him. However, after she had completed her studies and gained employment in a Child Care Centre in Bathurst, she had moved into town to be closer to her work.

Jimba had missed her very much. Though she had often sought him out when she visited her father at Barons Reach, it hadn't been the same as when she had been still living there. The weekends had dragged for him, and he had missed her company. However, when Libby began to visit Barons Reach, a completely new phase in his life, began.

Libby slows her stride as she approaches the front gate of the house. It looks different to how she remembers it, but she can't put her finger on it. She opens the gate to the house yard and walks up the path to the front door. She knocks softly at first, but again, more loudly, in an attempt to still her trembling hands. *Why am I nervous?* she asks herself. *I'm only here to talk to an old friend.*

The door opens and a young woman smiles at her. "Hello," she says brightly.

Libby is momentarily stunned, and stares at the slim woman with short dark curly hair and sea-green coloured eyes, smiling at her. However, when the woman's smile begins to wane and her eyebrows arch, inquisitively, Libby finally manages to speak.

"Oh, I'm sorry. I must have the wrong house."

Libby turns and begins to walk briskly down the path to the gate.

"No problem. Can I help you though?"

Turning around to acknowledge her, Libby notices she seems to look slightly amused.

"I mean, who are you looking for? I know everyone who lives at Barons Reach," she adds, with an even bigger smile than before.

"No, but thanks anyway," Libby calls back, as she closes the gate behind her and walks quickly away.

Libby now knows why the house yard looked different. When walking away, she had smelled the perfume from the young rose bushes positioned neatly around the perimeter of the house yard, and she had glanced at the fresh garden beds of lavender and bright coloured pansies. She had been too busy thinking about Jim to notice it before.

Who was that woman, and why was she living in Jim's house? Jim didn't have any other family than his father. At least, not when she had last been here. Could she be his sister? It was possible, she thinks. She looked to be around the same age as Jim, possibly a bit younger.

It then dawns on her that Jim may not live there anymore. He might only be helping with the tours, no longer living at Barons Reach. If she had asked Aunt Grace this morning, it would have saved her the embarrassment she just went through.

Well, it looks like she was not going to be able to speak to Jim in private this visit, but at least she might be able to speak to him tonight at the story-telling. She would just have to wait and see.

***

Libby had been right when she thought Mary and Grace wanted to have a mother – daughter talk. Grace began the discussion, although Mary had been expecting it.

"What am I going to do Mum?" Grace says, as she expels a huge sigh.

"I know it tough daughter, but I knows you'll do the right thing. Trouble is, sometimes I think you fighten' a curse this place got," she adds with a frown.

Grace looks out to the rolling green hills, patched with deep purple flowers, and wishes she could pretend her mother was talking about the Paterson's Curse weed. Well, that would be so much easier to fight, even as hard as it was to eradicate, she thinks.

"Hmm, I don't know Mum. Anyway, I thought we put all that behind us a long time ago. I mean look at what we've achieved the last twenty-five years. Think of everyone we've helped."

"Yeah, I know," Mary says, with a deep sigh of her own. "But, I don't like what this place has done to *you* daughter. It not right you had to suffer, and worry so."

Mary reaches for a tissue in the sleeve of her cardigan, dabs at her eyes and blows her nose.

Grace reaches over and pats her mother's arm. "It's ok Mum. Just wasn't meant to be," she says softly.

"No, it not ok," Mary says angrily. "No doubt about it, this place took your baby; my grandbaby. This place got a habit of takin' babies, alright."

Grace looks back out to the hills, deep in thought, while her mother regains control of her emotions. She doesn't need to respond to her mother's last words; they held - truth.

Could her mother be right though? Was this place also cursed?

She had married Dan a year after her brother, Darel and sister- in-law, Rachel, had been married by the river at Binda.

Darel and Rachel had been quickly blessed with a son, William, a year later. She had held her nephew in her arms, and from that moment, her arms had ached to hold a baby of her own.

Then Elizabeth was born, a few years later, and Grace still hadn't a baby of her own, although she had been thrilled for Darel and Rachel; two beautiful, healthy babies.

But, where was her baby? There was no reason she and Dan were not able to have children too. Her doctor had confirmed it through numerous tests. Patience!

Meanwhile, she remained an adoring aunt, spoiling her nephew and niece at every birthday and Christmas, and when they were school age, attending their sporting events and any school presentations.

She had given up her job at the Dubbo Medical Centre when she became the carer of Barons Reach. Suddenly, she was wealthy, and she hadn't needed to work. But she had then worked hard at setting things up for the visitor tours at Barons Reach, and applying herself to charity work in Dubbo.

She knew her nephew and niece so well, and loved them dearly. However, when she passed her twenty-ninth birthday, and she still hadn't fallen pregnant, she finally gave up hope that she would ever be able to hold a baby of her own in her arms.

She had poured her heart out to Dan about their childlessness; how she had wanted to give him a son or daughter. Typically, he had been her rock. He held her tenderly, told her that he had married her because he loved her and he wanted to spend the rest of his life with her. He said that if they were not able to have children, he would love her just the same.

One day though, he made the suggestion, that perhaps Barons Reach was her child; the way she applied herself so diligently and lovingly to every aspect of the property. If only he had known how those words would later haunt her, even though he had said them with no ill intent.

However, for a while his words were forgotten when her regular bleeding stopped, and her doctor confirmed her first pregnancy.

She had been unable to contain the joy she had felt during those first few weeks, and an almost uncontainable energy that seemed to stem from the essence of the new life within her. She had wanted to skip as she walked, and even contemplated running up the nearest hill when at Barons Reach, to shout the news of her impending motherhood to the world.

Despite her doctor's reassurance that she had in no way caused it, she still held doubt. Perhaps she had been *too* active. Maybe she should not have made all those trips to Barons Reach, in those first few weeks, and kept up her charity work at Dubbo. Could it have been too much on her body, for her baby, even though she could not dispute the science and wisdom of her doctor's medical knowledge and experience?

Perhaps Dan and her mother had been right. She had even lost her baby while she had been at Barons Reach. She would never forget - the pain in her heart when she discovered she had miscarried; the despair and grief that had followed; her mother's arms as she wept bitterly.

Had the ghosts of Barons Reach been jealous of the new life in her womb, wanted her all to themselves, because she had already given so much of herself to them and unconsciously made Barons Reach her baby? Was she, therefore, still responsible for her baby's death? Maybe she hadn't deserved to be a true mother, she had even thought.

Sometimes it did feel like she fought ghosts. She couldn't deny a certain obsession she had for Barons Reach. When she was back in Dubbo, her mind was often on the property, sometimes even in her dreams. And from the moment she passed through the front gates of Barons Reach each time, it was almost as if Old Mrs Bartlett was by her side, prompting her to immediately attend to its needs, as any mother should. Perhaps the battles of old, between the whites and the Wiradjuri, were still being waged in the spiritual world on Barons Reach, and as the current carer, she was the recipient of their wrath.

Nevertheless, she eventually accepted that Barons Reach was her baby. That there would be no other. Therefore, as a responsible parent, she ensured her baby was well looked after when she wasn't around.

Bill Sutton had been the Property Manager for more than twenty years when she took over Barons Reach. He'd had the place running like clockwork, so at first she'd been able to focus entirely on preparing Barons Reach for the visitor tours she and her mother planned. Dan's assistance had been invaluable; his knowledge of the building process, and his contacts through his work at the Dubbo Council in collaboration with the Bathurst Council.

Those first five years had been such busy years; planning, building, preparing and enacting the visitor tours. The family had rallied around her with encouragement and support, and she had felt such satisfaction, especially in the joy it had given her mother.

During the next five years, the bookings for the visitor tours to Barons Reach increased, along with her charity work at Dubbo. Libby began coming with them for the tours, and she had grown so fond of Barons Reach, and Jimba. It had also been during that time that she had lost Dan's baby, and finally accepted that it had been her destiny all along, to be the mother of Barons Reach.

However, when she passed her thirty-ninth birthday, she began to wonder what would happen to Barons Reach, once she died. Normally, she would leave the property to her children or another family member, in her Will.

Dan's only brother had no children either, but she wouldn't have felt right in entrusting Barons Reach to anyone without Wiradjuri heritage. She had sacrificed too much to do that, and it would not have been respectful to her mother, even if she had already passed by then.

She had even considered relinquishing Barons Reach, before she died, because as much as Barons Reach held her heart, her husband held it more, and her home was in Dubbo with her husband and where her family lived close by. She was realistic enough to know that in her later years, she would not be able to conduct visitor tours anymore. Wasn't it already too much for her mother? But, who would love her as much as she had.

She had pondered on this question for a long time, until one day, she looked out the kitchen window and noticed ten-year-old Libby and Jimba, racing off into the hills, and it came to her…

If she couldn't provide her own children for Barons Reach, then it should be children who already knew her and loved her, who would bring joy, hope, and the promise of a long life to the land.

Perhaps, she thought, somewhat sadly, she hadn't been meant to provide her own children for Barons Reach, with Bartlett blood in their veins. Maybe she had only been meant to return the land to the children of Wiradjuri heritage.

Libby loved her home at Binda, but everyone knew that both Binda and Jannali would eventually end up with her brother, Will, when both his grandparents and parents passed. He was their only grandson and son.

She had decided, there and then, that Libby would be the new mistress of Barons Reach one day. But, then she left and didn't return. And, Grace worried so…

Now, Libby is back! What is in store for her though? She is a beautiful and sweet young woman, bound to have men chasing her and wanting her for their wife. When Grace had chosen her, she had been so concerned with what was best for Barons Reach, she had not taken into consideration, Libby's ties to Dubbo. Would she want what could easily become a burden to her, if her heart were not in it like Grace's was, and especially if she married locally in Dubbo?

Mercifully, Libby had not had to experience anything like her grandmother and aunt had in their younger years. She had been spared, growing up around family who loved her dearly, on the land of her birth. But it had been because of her grandmother's and aunt's heartbreaking experiences that Barons Reach had become the haven and place of healing, that was now so well known.

Would Libby *want* to carry on for them, even if she never married? She has known about her Wiradjuri heritage from the time she could comprehend it, and she had practically been her grandmother's full-time student. Surely she wouldn't have taken to it so well, if she had not been meant to continue in her grandmother and aunt's footsteps. She had always been keen to learn about the Wiradjuri ways, and eager to come with her grandmother to Barons Reach. Grace wants to believe that it hadn't only been because of Jim. She still has - hope.

"You knew before I did, didn't you – about Libby?" Grace says, and turns to her mother.

"Yeah, it right, daughter."

"But do you think she'll want to? I mean, she was away for ten years, and she's only back now because we need her help."

Grace looks back out to the hills.

"Damn shame what happened to that dog," Mary says softly.

"Should we have told her what happened to Jim, do you think?"

"No daughter, that something she has ta find out for herself."

"I guess you're right. I just felt so rotten for not believing her at the time. But I didn't want to bring it back up again, later. She had been so upset. I didn't want to open old wounds," Grace says, turning back at her mother. "And poor Jim," she says, looking down at her hands interlocked in her lap, thoughtfully.

"Yeah, that boy more her best friend than she even know," Mary responds. "A good thing ya got rid of that mongrel."

Grace looks up suddenly. "Yes! If only I had known…better late than never I guess, though." Grace says, with a despondent sigh. "But I was sorry to see Bill go. He was a good man."

"Yeah, but giving Luke the job, the best thing ya coulda done. Now he getting' on, there's – Jim," Mary says, now smiling brightly.

Grace looks at her mother, thoughtfully. "You really think Jim's the one, for Libby?"

"Oh daughter, when I ever wrong?" Mary replies, and as if by mutual consent, they both stand and go into the house.

***

"So, it looks like you're the new story-teller now?" Jim says quietly to Libby, while Grandma Mary is engrossed in a conversation, with an older couple squatting beside her camp chair.

Libby and Jim have taken a few steps away from the trio. It had been difficult to hear what Jim was saying over her grandmother's excited voice anyway. It had been a good excuse to move away, and Libby is grateful to the couple talking to her grandmother. The woman had also been at the Home that Grandma Mary had been taken to, all those years ago, and had recognised her. They had a lot to talk about.

"Yes, well it sort of took me by surprise. I thought I was just here to help Grandma get around. That sort of thing," she says, looking over at her grandmother. "She's getting old you know," she adds, as if only realising that fact herself."

She turns back to Jim. He is looking at her as if he wants to say something, but something is holding him back.

"You don't live here, at Barons Reach, anymore?" she blurts out.

He looks at her confused. "No, yes, I mean – yes, I still live here. Why did you think I didn't?"

Libby is now nonplussed, but she doesn't want Jim to know she went looking for him.

"Oh, I just thought that maybe you were working somewhere else now, and just came back to help out with the tours."

"No, I've never left. I guess Barons Reach is my home…" He begins, turning his head slightly, looking away from her. Libby can now see his face more clearly in the fire light. She holds her breath as she watches him look out into the shadowed gums, "…as long as your aunt wants me, anyway," he concludes, turning back to her.

"What happened to your face Jim?" Libby asks, without thinking, reaching up and hesitantly touching the small scar she had noticed under his eye, when he had been looking away.

She can see sadness in his eyes as he reaches up and takes her hand, gently pulling it away and letting it go.

"Just something that happened a long time ago," he says, brushing it off, with an unconvincing grin.

His grin dissipates as he looks down, as if in deep thought. When he looks back up, he smiles softly, looking deeply into her eyes. "It was worth it though."

Libby doesn't know where to look when he looks at her that way. It makes her heart beat faster and her skin tingle. But, she doesn't want to feel that way - not now, not yet. She still has things she has to work out. And, why was it that it didn't feel like they were just friends anymore? It was like their relationship had changed, and while he seemed to know it, she didn't. When did that happen? She wasn't sure she wanted to be that way with him.

The truth of it was, she was a bit frightened by what she might find out. He said he still lived at Barons Reach, but who was that woman in his house? And how did he get that scar? She would have never imagined him to be a fighter, but she could see that even though small, that scar had once been a very deep cut. If he hadn't been in a fight she was sure he would have told her how he had got it. And the way he said, 'It was worth it though,' didn't sound like it had been an accident of some kind. Who was this man? Did she really know him, after all?

Libby turns to see the old couple saying goodbye to her grandmother. She is now relieved. She has an excuse to leave. She needs to be alone - to think, before she says anything more to Jim.

"Well, looks like it's time to go. I'm glad we ran into each other again," she says, wondering if she really is.

Once again, Jim seems to understand what she is really thinking, and she can see sadness appear in his eyes.

"Yes, me too. Take care Libby," he says softly, turns and walks away.

CHAPTER 9

Libby walks into her unit and closes the door behind her. She takes a deep breath and expels it, then begins unpacking her belongings.

The three women left Barons Reach that morning, as soon as they had ensured everything was back in its rightful place.

Aunt Grace had contracted cleaners for the upstairs of the house, where the house tours were conducted, but she took care of the bottom section of the house, where the family stayed when they visited.

Although Grandma Mary hadn't been able to help much with any of the physical tasks, she had been more than able to help with issuing orders to Libby.

It had been ten years since Libby was last in the house, but she had only been a child at the time, and hadn't been expected to do anything much apart from keeping the room in which she slept, tidy.

Now, as a young woman, things were much different. Her aunt and grandmother asked for her help, and she didn't mind at all. It felt good to be needed.

However, she had been eager to get back to her unit. She wanted to be around her familiar environment, so she could completely relax and think things through, about Jim.

She had enjoyed being back at Barons Reach. She had forgotten how beautiful the land was there; the lush rolling green hills, hugging valleys of tall timbers, lining the sparkling waters of the river. So picturesque! And – Murruway, standing so grand, a symbol of solidity and endurance. It had been difficult not to feel a sense of pride in the knowledge that she was still part of it all, even though she had turned her back on it for so long. Her grandmother and aunt had reassured her that she still had a place there, by their actions. Her grandmother first, by asking her to do the story-telling, followed by her aunt allowing her to do the upstairs house tour.

At the end of the second night, her grandmother said she sounded like she had been doing the story-telling for years. Perhaps she should have been, she had later thought. But even if she narrated the dreaming stories well, there was still so much more that her grandmother could contribute, as she had been doing for so many years.

Grandma Mary often spoke to the visitors before and after each story. They had lots of questions. Some wanted to know more about the Wiradjuri ways, and many had wanted to know if Mary had remembered their mothers, aunts or sisters. Mary had a long memory, and it surprised Libby by how much she remembered from her younger days.

Her grandmother had chatted a lot on the way home from Barons Reach. It had been a complete reversal to her closed eyes on the way there. The tours seemed to revitalise her emotionally, even if they tired her out physically. Perhaps it was just that the fall had taken more out of her than anyone realised, although Libby reminded herself that they had both been ten years younger when they had last been together at Barons Reach.

Grandpa Don was at the homestead when they arrived at Jannali. He still did some farming, but he had slowed down a lot over the last few years. He had recently turned seventy-nine, and finally accepted that some things were a bit beyond him now.

Libby's father and brother might live and work next door, but there wasn't a day that went by when one of them wasn't doing something at Jannali too. They all knew that the two properties would end up as her father's, and he would pass one of them on to her brother. It was a natural course.

Grandpa Don was obviously happy to see Grandma Mary, and he pecked her on the cheek as soon as she alighted from the car. Libby smiled with delight when she looked in the rear vision mirror as she was driving away, and saw her grandparents walk into the homestead holding hands.

***

"What were you dreaming about last night?" Teagan asks Libby as they sit on the lounge in the open spaced, lounge, dining and kitchen area of their unit.

It was Tuesday night, and they had hardly seen each other since Friday morning. Libby had already packed what she would need for Barons Reach in her car on Friday morning before work. That way, she had been able to go directly from her workplace to collect her grandmother at Jannali, back through Dubbo and on to Barons Reach. As planned, she didn't arrive back in Dubbo until Monday afternoon.

Teagan had then breezed into the unit after she had finished work, but she had left a few minutes later, after a quick change of clothes, hugging Libby as she swept out the door. Nick, her boyfriend, was on his way to pick her up. He had footy training on Monday nights, and Teagan sometimes went and watched, like the devoted girlfriend she was.

Libby was in bed by the time she returned, and they had both been running late for work this morning because they had overslept. So this was the first time they had really been together in over four days.

"Why? Was I talking in my sleep?" Libby replies.

"You sure were. I almost got out of bed to check on you. It must have been a nightmare. You sounded upset."

"Hmm, well, I can't really remember it," she replies, trying to look convincing.

In truth, she remembered a great deal of it. She had even woken herself up because she had been yelling.

In her dream, she had seen Jim's face in the distance, as she had last seen him, with the scar on his face. Then, all of a sudden, she was trying to swim upstream in the river, to Barons Reach, but the current had been so strong it had kept pulling her back downstream. It had seemed to have hands, gripping onto her, and she had fought to free herself from their hold. She became so tired though, she thought she was going to drown, and when she looked down, she saw Roger's face. That was probably when she had yelled out. She remembers hearing herself say, 'Nooo, Nooo,' as she was waking up.

"How did it go at Barons Reach?" Teagan asks, after swallowing a mouthful of warm milo, and looking at Libby over the rim of the mug.

"Yeah, good thanks. It was really nice to be able to spend some time with Aunt Grace and Grandma," she replies, glancing at the television. "How was your weekend? What did you get up to?" she adds, attempting to change the subject.

"Oh, Nick and I went to the Club on Friday night. We sat with Chloe, Jason and Matt. There was a disco. It was okay. Then I hung around at work on Saturday, waiting for Steph to finish. We then went and watched Nick and Tom at the footy. They won. Nick came over Saturday night and then I hung out with Cloe, Jason and Matt on Sunday. We watched some DVD's. I hope I didn't wake you when I got home last night."

"You never disturb me," Libby replies, smiling at her friend.

In truth, Libby had heard Teagan arrive, but she didn't let her know she was awake. It was late and they both had work in the morning. She knew Teagan would be full of news about her weekend, and she had had enough on her mind as it was. That was why she had still been awake; tossing and turning, thinking about Barons Reach and Jim.

"By the way…" Teagan begins, waiting for Libby to look at her. "Matt said to say 'hello'." She grins at Libby and rolls her eyes.

Libby rolls her eyes back.

"Well, you know he has a thing for you. And he's a really sweet guy. I don't know why you don't want to go out with him. What is it you don't like about him?" she asks, arching her eyebrows.

"Oh Teagan, I don't know. It's just…" she begins, but she doesn't know how to explain it, so she just shrugs her shoulders.

She really likes Matt, but it just doesn't feel right to encourage him. He is the elder brother of their friend, Chloe, and the girls have known him since High School. Towards the end of her final year, he had started to take every opportunity to talk to her, and ever since they had left school, he always seemed to be around whenever she and Teagan were with Chloe.

"Well, if you really don't like him, *I* might be interested," Teagan says, looking down into her mug, swirling the dregs of her drink before emptying it all into her mouth, and swallowing it with a final gulp.

"*Teagan!*" Libby declares, surprised by her friends words. "But, what about Nick?"

Teagan grimaces, and answers Libby's questioning look. "We had a fight after the footy on Saturday. I'm just so tired of him always wanting to go off with his footy mates, *every* Saturday night."

"But didn't you just say he came here on Saturday night?

"Yeah, but only after he'd had about a dozen drinks at the pub. He was plastered by then, of course. At least he had the sense to get dropped off, but I had to take him home, after he woke up. We were snuggled-up on the lounge watching a movie on telly, but he fell asleep nearly as soon as it started. I just don't know if I want to put up with it anymore."

Teagan stands, and takes her mug to the kitchen. Libby can see she is holding back tears. Libby follows her to the kitchen. She walks over and stands beside her friend, waiting while she rinses out her mug. Then she wraps her arms around her in a hug. Teagan begins to cry on her shoulder.

"Have you talked to him about it?" Libby asks, as they disengage and Teagan reaches for a tissue from the box on the counter.

"Yeah, well I've let him know how I feel about it, that's for sure."

Libby suddenly has an idea that might help her friend.

"Hey, would you like to come with me next weekend? I have to drive my grandmother to Barons Reach, for another visitor tour that's booked."

Teagan stops mopping her eyes and looks at Libby thoughtfully.

"You know, that would be kinda cool. Have a sorta girl's weekend away," she says, a thoughtful expression now replacing the previous downcast one.

"Yeah, well, I'll be kinda busy helping my grandmother. But, you might find it interesting, and maybe Nick will start to think about things more seriously if you aren't around next weekend. I'll have to ask my aunt first of course, but I'm sure she won't mind."

"I don't know if it will make any difference. To Nick, I mean. But, I'd like to come with you." Teagan says, now looking so much brighter. "Thanks Libby," she says, reaching forward and giving her a big hug.

✳✳✳

As Libby lies in bed that night, she thinks about her earlier conversation with Teagan.

She understands why Teagan is upset about Nick's drinking. It isn't just on Saturday nights. He is rarely sober whenever she sees him at the Club, or one of the pubs in town, when she goes out. Most of her friends enjoy a social drink when they are out, but they don't get as drunk as Nick does, *every* time.

She overindulged one night, and woke up with a throbbing headache and only a poor memory of the previous night. But she had never repeated the experience. Of course, she could have blamed Teagan for that night, encouraging her to match her, drink for drink, but she knew she had only herself to blame.

The boys, however, were much more regular in their drinking habits. It was like it was almost expected of them to spend a great deal of their time at the pub, as some of their father's did. It was a meeting place, like the Club, but whereas the Club was more a meeting place for both genders, the pubs were more male-orientated, and more frequently visited by the boys. For them, going to the pub was quite a regular occurrence on a Saturday night, especially after a sporting event. They would either mutually celebrate a victory, or drown their sorrows if they had lost.

She knew Teagan understood why Nick went to the pub after playing a football match, and of all people, she could relate to wanting to celebrate. She would rarely pass up an invitation to party, and she could party with the best of them. In so many ways, they were very alike. However, Teagan didn't always overdo it with alcohol. Unfortunately, Nick obviously just didn't know when to stop.

She considers the phrase, 'opposites attract'. Could that be Teagan and Nick's downfall – that they were *too* alike? It makes so much more sense though, that people would be attracted to others with similar thought patterns and interests. However, although the same gender, her friendship with Teagan was proof that opposites attract, so perhaps there was some truth to it.

She still finds it difficult to imagine Teagan with Matt though. He couldn't be more different to Nick, and Teagan had obviously found Nick's quick wit, competitive nature, love of sport and being outdoors, appealing, to become his girlfriend in the first place. Matt, on the other hand, was the complete opposite. He preferred being indoors and largely kept to himself, a self-professed bookworm. Matt had often talked to Libby about books, and his favourite authors. He was always interesting to talk to, and she enjoyed their conversations. In several respects, he was a lot like Libby, although Libby preferred being outside than indoors. So, she reconsiders. Perhaps the phrase 'opposites attract', doesn't hold much merit after all. Yet, she wasn't interested in Matt, romantically, anyway, for all that she liked about him, including his looks. He is quite good looking, she admits, although not anywhere near as handsome as Jim.

Well, she couldn't help but compare him to Jim. However, there was a huge difference there, too. Though Matt was a few years older than she was, and Jim, she still thought of him as a boy. However, she could never think of Jim anymore as a boy, even though she had kept an image of him as a ten year old in her mind, until she had seen him recently.

No, when she saw Jim in her mind now, he was definitely a – man. And he made her feel like a woman, not a girl. She tries to remember when that had happened. Had it been at the touch of his hand, when he had moved her fingers away from the small scar on his cheek? Or, had it been even before that, when he had looked deeply in to her eyes. Perhaps it had been from the first sight of his outline in the shadows on the other side of the fire. She remembers she had felt not only curious, but compelled, to keep her eyes on him, then.

She had initially only hoped, if she saw him again, to be able to attain a peaceful resolution with him for her past action. If only she hadn't felt that instant attraction. She would have been able to talk to him as a friend, without the butterflies. She would have been able to ask him outright about that woman in his house, and she would most likely be able to forget about that scar. It was his business after all, and even though she had once been his best friend, it had been long ago.

But, was that a valid reason not to care about him anymore? Even if she didn't feel the way she did about him now, she could, and should, still care about him as a friend. She may not have acted like a friend by turning her back on him so long ago, but that was the past, and she had to forgive herself for that. She was trying to make amends, after all, wasn't she? So she should be concerned about him; perhaps, not about that woman, but at least about his response to her question about the scar.

If it had resulted from carelessness, surely he would have told her. If he had done something silly, when they were younger, he had always been able to laugh at himself. On the other hand, if he had been in an accident of some kind, surely he could have just told her. She would have readily offered sympathy. But, he had just sadly said, *'it was worth it though'*, when she had asked. It troubled her.

Did he now have anger issues? Had he been in a fight with someone, and if he had, how had his opponent faired? She finds it hard to imagine anyone getting the better of Jim, now. He had never been like that when he was a boy, always good-natured, and she can't remember him ever being unkind, or even - angry. But, maybe he wasn't like that anymore.

Why did she feel he was being secretive about it though?

Her thoughts seem to keep returning to Jim, with no definite resolution, so she tries to think of something else.

She is glad Teagan is coming with her next weekend. She has shown a lot of interest in Barons Reach and the tours, ever since she told her about it all. She thinks Teagan will enjoy the experience. Both her grandmother and aunt have known her since she had been in High School with Libby, so she is sure they won't mind her visiting.

Hopefully, the break from Nick will help their relationship too. 'Absence makes the heart grow fonder', as they say, so Libby is hoping the time apart for Teagan and Nick, will give them both time to think more clearly about their situation.

If only she had thought more clearly, before staying away from Barons Reach for ten years. She had certainly taken it to the extreme. It had not been ideal, resolved anything, and only resulted in a new problem for her.

If she had been able to let go of her hate for Roger, as her grandmother had suggested, she wouldn't have missed out on all those years of friendship with Jim. She is sure now that she would never have remained mad at him, if she had returned to Barons Reach earlier. She would have noticed if he changed, and she most likely wouldn't have this current dilemma.

But, if he *has* changed - why?

CHAPTER 10

"Oh *wow*," Teagan whispers, looking out the side-window, clearly astonished.

Libby smiles to herself as she looks in the rear-vision mirror at her friend in the back seat of the car. She can see that Teagan's eyes are glued to the stately looking house of Barons Reach.

Libby turns the car off the road, through the front gates, and follows the road up to the house, to the garage behind it. She switches the ignition off.

"Gosh Libby," Teagan says, looking at the imposing structure beside the car, with wide-open eyes. "This place is a mansion."

Libby laughs. "Yes, I used to call it that too."

Aunt Grace appeared in front of the car then, and after welcoming them all, helped carry some of their belonging to their bedrooms. Then they all went to the kitchen.

Aunt Grace had a cup of tea ready for Grandma Mary. She said she had noticed Libby's car coming up the front drive and put the kettle on. She asked Teagan if she would like tea or coffee tea, but Libby interjected.

"Hot Milo for Teagan also, please Aunt Grace."

"Would that be Libby's influence, by any chance?" she then asked

Teagan.

"Yep, she converted me," Teagan replied, smiling.

Aunt Grace looked back at Libby and smiled softly. Libby's fondness for Milo always reminded her of her mother. Rachel's favourite beverage had always been hot Milo when she was Libby's age too."

When Aunt Grace confirmed that it would be fine for Teagan to come to Barons Reach with Libby for the next visitor tour, Libby filled her friend in about the general tour itinerary.

"But, I'll be busy helping Grandma a lot, so I might not attend everything. It just depends on how Grandma is," she told her. "You'll be a guest too, so you're not expected to do anything, of course," she added.

Teagan was quick to reply she would be happy to help in any way, all the same, and that Libby just needed to ask.

Libby was glad to see that her friend had cheered up a bit by coming with her to Barons Reach. Although avoidance wouldn't necessarily fix the issue she had with her boyfriend, at least her friend now had some time-out from mulling over it, as she had been doing all week.

The sun had been setting as they had arrived, so by the time they settled in and tidied up after the evening meal, it was well and truly dark outside. They all moved to the lounge room, to relax.

Grandma Mary settled herself in her favourite comfy lounge chair. Aunt Grace took the matching lounge chair, and the two younger women, nestled into the wide, three-seater lounge, in between.

Grandma Mary picked up the remote control for the television, on the side-table beside her, and turned it on. She began surfing the channels, finally stopping on a station airing the movie, 'Cold Mountain', starring Nicole Kidman.

They all watched it for a few minutes, but then Aunt Grace said she had already seen the movie, and she had office work that needed her attention. She bade everyone goodnight, in case they were in bed when she came back out, excused herself, and walked out.

Libby could see Teagan wasn't at all interested in watching television, because she couldn't stop looking around at everything.

"I'll show you upstairs, tomorrow," Libby says, gaining Teagan's attention. "I'd show you now but it looks better during the day. The view is amazing from the master bedroom."

"No worries. Sounds great," Teagan replies.

Grandma Mary closes her eyes. Libby moves over to her and gently touches her arm.

"You ok Grandma?" she asks.

Grandma Mary opens her eyes. "Yes granddaughter, but I think I might go to bed. Leave you two young'uns to it," she says, casting a small smile Teagan's way, and rising from her chair. She begins slowly making her way to the door.

"Do you need a hand, Grandma? Libby asks.

"No granddaughter, I fine. See ya both in the mornin'."

"Night Grandma," Libby replies.

"Goodnight Mr's Rutherford," Teagan adds.

"Goodnight," Grandma Mary says, halfway through the door.

Though her leg is much better now, she still limps a little, and Libby found out today that she is still missing her independence. She made that clear when Libby picked her up at Jannali earlier that afternoon.

"I can manage walkin' now granddaughter. I can at least do that," she said, when Libby attempted to help her walk to the car from the homestead. However, despite her words spoken a little gruffly, Libby knew it was that she had just been a bit frustrated by not being able to do the things she normally did anymore. So, she just walked behind her, and watched her closely.

Libby jumps up from the lounge and turns the television off. It was a good movie. She knew, because she and Teagan had hired it out from the DVD shop a few months ago. If she had been back at her unit she would probably have watched it again, but they had missed the beginning, and Libby preferred watching movies from the beginning, even if she had already seen them. Besides, she could easily see Teagan hadn't been interested. Motioning to her with her hand, she walks towards the hallway.

"Come on, I want to show you something."

Teagan follows Libby to the library, next to the office where Aunt Grace is working. The library is practically sound proof, so Libby is not concerned they will disturb her aunt.

She turns to watch her friend's face as she follows her footsteps into the room.

"Oh, you're kidding me," Teagan says, her mouth agape.

Bookcases fill two sides of the room, from the floor to the ceiling, and an upright piano rests, angled, at the far windows.

"How do you get a book from up there?" Teagan asks, looking up and craning her neck as high as she can at the rows of leather bound books, doubt written all over her face.

Libby points to the corner of the room, closest to the hallway, at a massive big wooden ladder.

"No way!" she exclaims, looking at Libby.

Libby giggles, giving it away.

"No, we use this now," she says, pointing to a sturdy looking metal stepladder in the opposite corner, with wheels at the bottom that roll along the floorboards. "But, they used to use that one…" she says pointing back to the wooden ladder, "…before my aunt installed that one," she concludes, pointing to the steel ladder again. "Apparently one of the domestics fell from the wooden one while she was dusting the bookshelves up there," she says, pointing up to the top shelf of books.

"What happened to her?" Teagan asks, looking shocked.

"Aunt Grace said she wasn't sure, but I reckon she would have died. I can't imagine anyone surviving a fall like that. Aunt Grace probably knows what happened to her, but she didn't want to tell me, upset me. I think she just wanted to make sure I never used that ladder."

"Well, I bet it worked. Mind you, if it weren't for your love of books, I couldn't imagine you would attempt it anyway. You're usually pretty cautious about things," Teagan says, stirring her.

Libby takes the joke while feigning a look of affront, but then she nods her head sadly, accepting the truth of the words.

"Hey girlfriend, I didn't mean to offend you," Teagan adds, looking a little concerned.

"I know," Libby replies, walking over to the piano and sitting on the piano-seat. She turns in the seat, toward the windows, lifts the heavy emerald green velvet drape to the side, and looks out into the night. "It's true though, you're right. I am very cautious; about - everything."

Teagan walks over to Libby and puts her arm over her shoulder.

"What's going on, hey? Want to talk about it? she asks, quietly.

Libby lets the drape fall back to its original position, and turns to look at her friend.

"No, I'm fine," she says with a forced smile. "Nothing to worry about."

"You sure?" Teagan asks, looking dubious.

"Yeah, I'm good," she responds, and then yawns. "Sorry," she says, while stifling it. "Had a hectic day at work – week, actually."

"Yeah, I know. I'm still not used to standing all day," Teagan says, offhandedly.

"Well, I certainly shouldn't complain, sitting down most days," Libby offers, feeling guilty for mentioning it in the first place.

"Yeah, but you do all that mental stuff," Teagan adds with a grin.

"Well, anyway, I think we've both talked ourselves into going to bed," Libby says, as she stands up and walks towards the door.

"I reckon," Teagan replies, following her, and yawning.

***

The next morning, after breakfast, as she had said she would the previous night, Libby took Teagan to the upstairs of the house.

Teagan was fascinated by everything she saw, and she said she felt like she was in a castle. Libby had laughed when she said that, and then told Teagan how she had once asked Aunt Grace if she were a queen, for that very reason.

As it was a beautiful spring morning, the two young women decided to go for a walk. Libby said she would show Teagan some of her favourite places. She decided she would start with the river.

Teagan follows Libby out the garden gate and catches up to her, to walk beside her.

As they walk along the path that Libby and Jim had often used, Libby points in the directions of the gravesite they would visit after lunch and the story-telling fire-site that night.

"Of course, you don't have to come to either if you don't want to," Libby tells her as they walk along.

"But, I do," Teagan responds looking a little putout that Libby would think such a thing. "I may not have aboriginal blood, but I am really interested in your Wurr..." She frowns, attempting to say the word correctly.

"Wir-ad-ju-ri," Libby says for her.

"Yes, Wirad-juri, ancestors. And I find it all so interesting, you know, how your family is showing both sides of everything. You've got this incredible house that was the first one of its kind ever built in the area, and all that history it contains. Plus, you've got the gravesite of an amazing aboriginal warrior, who defended his country and tried to save his people, right here on this property - which, by the way, I'm really looking forward to seeing. And on top of all that, I get to sit around a fire and hopefully hear you tell some really fascinating stories, which have been passed down, from generation to generation for thousands…in fact, as you've taught me, for more than 40,000 years. Who wouldn't be interested?"

Libby stops walking and turns to look at her friend squarely, with a huge grin.

"Ok, I'm convinced," she says, giving Teagan a quick hug.

As they reach a rise on a grassy hill, they stop to catch their breath, and Libby points down to the river.

"It's so beautiful here, Libby. How come you haven't been back until last week? I mean ten years is a long time."

Teagan looks at her with a frown of confusion.

Libby wasn't expecting that question from Teagan, but she knows now, she should have been. She would have asked Teagan the very same question if things had been in reverse.

She had recently relived all the pain of that last day at Barons Reach when she had found that photo, but she has been through a great deal of soul-searching since then, and resolved quite a lot, she thinks. She would like to think she has put it all behind her.

The trouble is, because she had been away so long, she now had to sort out her current situation with Jim, and she was constantly reminded that it all stemmed from the fact that she had been away so long – because of that last day. So that last day still haunted her.

She has never spoken about it to anyone because she had not even wanted to think about it. But, she had been doing a great deal of thinking about it lately, and she still intends to apologise to Jim, if she can only find the right moment. Perhaps telling Tegan might, in some way, help her for when she does talk to Jim. Besides, if she wanted a good listener, she couldn't have a better one, than Teagan.

Teagan may never have been short of a word, a natural chatterbox, but along with learning the skills of a hairdresser, she had also learned how to be a good listener. Most women liked to talk to their hairdresser when they were having their hair, cut, styled or shampooed. Sometimes it was just to kill the time, but Libby felt a lot of it had to do with how relaxing the process was, prompting conversation. She liked going to the hairdressers. It felt like she was having her head massaged, as the hairdresser combed her hair in various directions to cut it. However, she wanted to keep her hair long, at least for now. She liked being able to put it up on occasions, although she preferred to allow it to fall wherever it liked. She would never mention that to Teagan though, because it would give her added leverage in attempting to coerce Libby to let her cut her hair.

Sometimes Teagan would tell Libby about something she had found out from a customer, but Libby also knew there were things about customers she would never repeat. She wasn't one to deliberately spread gossip. Libby knew Teagan kept confidences, and the only reason she hadn't told her about Barons Reach was because she had been trying to forget it.

"It's kind of a long story," she ventures, still a little hesitant about putting her experience into words.

"I've got all morning, it seems," Teagan replies, walking over to an outcrop of rocks. She sits on the grass in front of it, leans back, and pats the grass beside her, indicating she wants Libby to join her.

Libby sits beside her and begins her story. She tells Teagan about her friendship with Jim, and about Roger - what he had done to Tiger.

Teagan listened to every word, and the expression on her face changed several times while Libby told her story; from inquisitiveness to anger, and finally, sadness.

At the end of the story, Teagan moves closer to Libby and puts her arm around her shoulder, giving her a sideways hug.

"I'm so sorry," she says. "That must have been so awful, and especially when you were so young."

Libby accepts her friend's sympathy, but she is surprised to feel that it hasn't been as painful to tell as she had thought. It was as if her friend really had shared a part of the pain with her. She thinks of how her mother had often said, 'A problem shared, is a problem halved.' Perhaps it really was true.

Teagan moves back to her original spot and looks into Libby's face thoughtfully. "So, have you seen either of them since you've been back?"

Libby nods. "I've seen Jimba, that is – Jim, as he is now called. But, thankfully, not Roger."

Teagan looks closely into Libby's eyes, as she asks. "So, how was Jim when you saw him?"

"Ok, I guess."

Teagan looks at her with arched eyebrows and wide-open eyes.

"Is that all you're going to give me? Seriously?" she says, with feigned disapproval.

Libby chuckles. "Well, I see your point," she says, looking embarrassed. "No, he was fine. I mean, we talked." She pauses…

"Hmm? And?"

"Well it was a bit hard with Grandma right beside me. She even corrected me when I called him Jimba, instead of Jim. How was I supposed to know? And, he was so evasive about things."

"Such as?" Teagan prompts.

"Well…" Libby begins, but decides this is something she wants to work out herself, so she tries to end the discussion. "…he just didn't seem to want to tell me much about himself." She shrugs her shoulders. "It was probably just me. I don't know."

"Will he be at any of the things today?"

"Probably the story-telling, tonight. It seems he prepares the fire, like his father used to."

"Oh good. So I'll get to see him at least. So, what does he look like now?"

Libby was just about to say, '*you won't be able to miss him, he'll be the best looking man there,*' but she just manages to pull herself up in time.

"Oh, tall, sandy coloured hair and dark brown eyes."

CHAPTER 11

Libby tries to avoid looking to her left, on the far side of the fire, although she likes to scan the faces of the visitors as she speaks, as much as possible. She has found that individual visitors seemed to like it too, if she stopped and looked at them for a few seconds while talking, especially the children.

Grandma Mary asked her to tell all the dreaming stories tonight. She is really enjoying it, and she will enjoy telling this last one, most of all. She can imagine the children being tucked into their beds already, thinking about it, or even looking out at the night sky from their beds, if they are able to.

If only she knew what Jim had said to Teagan, and why Teagan was standing so close to that woman she had found at Jim's house last week. It is bothering her, even though it shouldn't, and that is why she is trying not to look at where the three stand, to her left, on the far side of the fire.

"What do you see, up there, in the night sky?" Libby asks the group around the fire, as she points up at the stars twinkling in the darkness. All faces instantly look up, and several young voices call out, 'the moon, the stars,' as she has anticipated. But a teenage voice adds proudly, 'the Southern Cross', as she had hoped.

"Well, you are *all* correct, but regarding the Southern Cross, that group of stars also has another name. A name it was called a very long time ago, before it was given the name of the Southern Cross. It was called, 'Mirrabooka', by the Wiradjuri people. And the reason it was given that name is because...

A long time ago, there was a very kind and wise man, named, Mirrabooka. Mirrabooka looked after his people so well that the Creator Spirit, 'Biyaami', decided to reward him by granting him eternal life once he died on earth. When that day came, Biyammi placed him in the sky and stretched him across it. And that is what you are looking at up there, that group of stars also known as, the Southern Cross – Mirrabooka!

Libby can't help but smile as she watches the faces look up again at the sky, and some of the children exclaim that they can see it now, after their parents point it out to them.

"And for those who know the stars well," she adds, and all the faces return to look at her again. "The two most prominent stars, known as, the Pointers, or Alpha and Beta Centauri, are really Mirrabooka's eyes – watching over the earth."

"Well that's it for tonight. Thank you for coming," she says, smiling, and the group begins to dissemble.

Libby can't help herself. She immediately looks over to the three figures she had tried to avoid looking at throughout the story-telling.

The last time she glanced that way, Teagan was standing between that woman and Jim, but now the woman is between Teagan and Jim, and she is saying something to him.

Teagan locks eyes with her, and grins mischievously.

"You did real good granddaughter. You a story-teller alright," her grandmother says softly, drawing her attention.

"Thanks Grandma. I really enjoy it. Did you see the look on the faces of the kids?"

"Yeah, it make you feel proud, alright," Mary replies.

Libby smiles at her, and then she spots someone walking over, looking at her grandmother. She can see she wants to talk to her, so she makes a move.

"I'll just be over there," she says, as she points to where Teagan, Jim and that woman are. "Be back soon," she adds, leaving her grandmother to her conversation with the woman standing beside her.

She makes her way around the fire, although slower than she expects, because several people stop her to thank her for her story-telling. Finally, she is standing beside Teagan.

"Hey, you're a natural," she says, smiling wide. "I had no idea you were also a teacher."

Libby offers her a smile of thanks, but she isn't able to avoid looking at the woman who has now moved towards her.

"We meet again," she says, with a forced smile on her face. Libby can see it is not sincere.

Libby glances at Jim. He looks at her as if he is deep in thought.

"Yes," Libby replies. "I'm Libby. And you are...?" she says, eager to know her name.

"Hanna," she replies, and her sea-green eyes bore into Libby's of sky-blue.

Libby looks back at Jim. He is glancing around at the stragglers of the group, departing. He looks like something is bothering him, but he could also just be bored, Libby decides.

"I think your grandmother is waiting Libby," he says, turning back to face her, and indicating with his head.

"She looks over to her grandmother, but she can see she is still talking to the woman she had left her with.

She frowns. Is he trying to get rid of her? Then she looks back at Hanna, who is now looking over at Jim with a wide grin. Well that confirms it. She suddenly feels embarrassed, and wants to get away. She looks at Teagan.

"Time to go, I reckon."

Teagan looks surprised, but nods.

"Well, nice to meet you, *properly*, Hanna, and to see you again, Jim," she forces out, unable to smile. She looks at each of them in turn, and begins to walk off, with Teagan beside her.

She is half-way around the fire, when Jim is suddenly by her side.

"Hey, I just wanted to say…you're really good at the story-telling. I hope you keep doing it," he says, looking strained.

Libby is still feeling bruised by the previous encounter, and although she appreciates his comment, she's determined she's not going to let on.

"I don't know now Jim," she replies. "I thought I was going to…"

she begins, and she can't help but glance at Hanna appearing at his side. "but...," she shrugs her shoulders, and walks away.

"See ya," Teagan says to Jim and Hanna, and follows Libby.

***

"I can tell you're mad Libby," Teagan says, as the two girls prepare for bed, after saying good night to Libby's grandmother and aunt.

"Yeah, well, it's something I'm used to being with Jim, it seems," she responds, pulling back the bedclothes and sliding between the sheets.

She closes her eyes immediately, pretending to fall asleep as Teagan climbs into the matching single bed beside her.

"Are you sure you don't want to talk about it," Teagan asks, hopefully.

"No, I'm fine," Libby replies curtly, but feeling a little guilty for snapping at her friend, adds, "Thanks all the same."

Teagan turns off the lamp on the table between them.

"You know, he's not interested in Hanna."

Libby opens her eyes and stares at the outline of her friend in the near darkness.

"What do you mean?" she asks, trying hard to keep control of her voice.

"Well, it was obvious to me. She kept trying to get his attention. But he only had eyes for you."

'Yeah, well, that's not what I saw," she answers, feeling even more deflated now. "Night," she says, trying to pretend she wasn't thinking about it anymore.

"Night girlfriend," Teagan says, with a sigh.

***

"Mum, please?" Libby begs, as she holds the mobile phone to her ear, and looks out at the river at her favourite park in Dubbo. "I'll even come out and spend the weekend at Binda, cook for Dad and Will, and check up on Grandpa," she adds.

There is silence down the line.

"Mum?"

"Yes, ok - but what happened darling? You know you can tell me," Rachel says, concern in her voice. "I thought you were enjoying your time with Grandma and Aunt Grace."

"Oh no, yes – I am. It's just that...I want to stay around Dubbo this weekend, that's all. I need some time...," she begins lamely.

"Yes, I'll go in your place this time Libby, but – I know there's something you're not telling me. I know more about things than you realise, you know," she says, an attempt to coerce Libby to talk, obvious.

Libby feels close to tears. She feels embarrassed by how she had reacted when she last saw Jim. She had already decided she was only going to be his friend, despite knowing how attracted she was to him in other ways. How could she have allowed her heart to rule her head, when the facts had been staring her in the face, all along? It was just that when she had come face-to-face with Hanna, she fully understood how strong her feelings really were for Jim. She just can't understand why she had allowed herself to be that way. How can she face him again, when she isn't able to control herself? She will just end up feeling wounded – again, although in a different way from all those years ago. Was it destined? Was she supposed to stay away, after all?

"Libby?" her mother says, and Libby realises she has been waiting for her to answer.

"Yes Mum, I'm here. I know. Thank you, but I just don't want to talk about it at the moment. Ok?"

"Ok darling, but remember, I may be your mother, but I've had my share of things to work out when I was your age too. I might be able to help."

"Yeah, I know Mum. Thanks. Please tell Grandma and Aunt Grace I'm sorry. I love you. Bye."

Libby hangs up and puts the phone beside her on the grass. She feels relieved now she doesn't have to go to Barons Reach this weekend, but also – sad, because she will miss being with her grandmother and aunt, and helping with the story-telling. She even enjoyed doing the house tour and if her aunt ever needed her to, she would eagerly do the gravesite readings as well.

She is becoming more and more, fond of Barons Reach, and Murruway, too. She thinks it strange that she is the only one in the family who calls the house by her rightful name.

She has come to think of both Barons Reach and Murruway as being female. It isn't because it has mostly only known female owners and occupants for most of the last hundred years. Although so grand looking from the outside, she finds that once she steps inside Murruway, she instantly feels soothed, protected. She also makes her feel calm and strong. Yet, here she was, deliberately staying away – again, when by all accounts, she now wanted to be there, so very much.

She stands and makes her way back to her car. She won't tell Teagan, doesn't need to. Teagan wasn't going to go with her to Barons Reach this weekend anyway, because she and Nick were going camping for the weekend. Just the two of them, he'd said. He didn't have to play footy on Saturday and he wanted to spend the whole weekend with Teagan. It seemed her idea had worked, and Nick had had time to think seriously about his relationship. Libby was happy for Teagan.

Besides, she would be going to Binda for the weekend to take care of meals for her father and brother, and check up on Grandpa Don. It will be peaceful there. A good place for her to do some serious thinking...

CHAPTER 12

Mary, Grace and Rachel, sit around the kitchen table drinking tea. Rachel and Mary arrived at Barons Reach about an hour ago, but Grace had arrived early that afternoon.

"She's runnin'," Mary says flatly. "Reminds me of her mother and aunt, 'bout the same age."

Rachel and Grace look at each other, with arched eyebrows and wide eyes, and nod at each other, confirming Mary's words.

"Yep, it seems so," Rachel then verbally confirms.

"I wish I knew what happened," Grace says, frowning. "I mean, she seemed to be really enjoying her time here since coming back. But she did seem keen to leave the morning after the last story-telling. Did something happen there Mum?"

Mary twists her mouth, as if literally, chewing on ideas. "Well, she ended up talking to Jim at the end, although Hanna was there, as well as Teagan. I don't know what was said, 'cause they were talkin' the other side of the fire."

"Who's Hanna?" Rachel asks abruptly, suddenly sensing something familiar about the situation.

Mary and Rachel both look at Grace, expectantly.

"Oh she's Pete's daughter. He started here about six months ago.

His wife left him and he wanted to start afresh. He turned up with Hanna after I gave him a job, so I put them both in the second family home. He had really good references, so I knew he'd be a good worker. It seems Hanna wanted to make sure he was ok, and look after him for a while. She gets on better with her father than her mother, apparently. She's got a job in town, but lives here."

"So of course, Jim and Luke are now in the Manager's house," Rachel adds, half to herself.

Grace nods.

Rachel is gathering facts. She feels she needs to have a good heart-to-heart with her daughter. Something doesn't feel right about her not wanting to come back all of a sudden, this time. Last time it was clear it was because of Tiger dying, but she had only been a child then. She is a young woman now.

"It's probably to do with this – Hanna." Rachel states.

Mary and Grace look up at her.

"That's what I reckon, anyway," Rachel says looking back into her teacup.

"I think you onta something there," Mary says, nodding.

"Well, the thing is, is Jim interested in Hanna?" Rachel asks Grace.

Grace frowns, thinking hard. "Well, I don't see them much you know, the workers, so I don't really know."

Rachel looks at Mary.

"Was this Hanna at all the story-telling's?"

Mary sighs. "No, just the last one. Yep, that gotta be it, 'cause Jim and Libby seem fine with each other again, till she poked her head in."

Rachel nods. "Well, I'll have a good talk to her when I go back. If she now had feelings for Jim, and knows for sure that he likes Hanna, then I guess it's understandable that she feels uncomfortable. But – if she's just trying to run away, and doesn't know for sure, then…"

"She come back. I know it. Just a hiccup this time," Mary states.

Grace sighs and Rachel looks at her.

"Well, I hope you're right Mum," Grace replies, and suddenly Grace and Rachel smile, as they say in unison, with Mary, "When I ever wrong?"

Mary looks fondly on her daughter and daughter-in-law. "'Bout time you know it."

***

Libby has just finished tidying up the kitchen when Rachel walks through the door. Libby had heard her drive up a few moments ago.

"Hi Mum, you're back. Did you have a good trip?" she asks, as she walks over and pecks her on the cheek.

"Yes, thanks darling," Rachel replies, returning the kiss, depositing her handbag on the kitchen table, and her overnight bag on the floor nearby. "I imagine you'll want to get going soon, so this can wait," she says, indicating her overnight bag. "Let's have a cuppa," she adds, looking pointedly at Libby as she pulls out a chair and sits.

Libby is puzzled by that look her mother just gave her. Her mind flies in every direction as she walks over and turns on the electric kettle on the kitchen counter. She had just filled it with water a few moments ago. She opens a cupboard door above the kettle and takes out the milo her mother keeps there for her when she visits. She then opens the adjoining cupboard and chooses two mugs, placing them beside the tea bag tin, sugar bowl and milo. Finally, she takes the milk from the fridge as the kettle switches off, and Rachel begins…

"I want to tell you something, but I don't want you to think I'm having a go at you or trying to sway you, ok?"

Libby nods, a small frown appearing on her brow, and leans back against the sink, crossing her arms.

Rachel instantly notices Libby is in defence mode. *I probably should have started differently*, she thinks, and changes course…

"When I was about your age, I almost made a huge mistake," she begins. "I almost lost both your father and Binda."

Libby remains in her position, but her face now relaxes, softens.

"In fact, I thought I really only loved Binda," she says, with sad eyes. "And then I made the mistake of thinking your Aunt Grace was, well, your father's lover. She was living at Binda with him at the time."

Grace watches her daughter move towards her and sit next to her, the tea and milo making, now completely forgotten. She looks puzzled.

"But, how could you have thought that?" she asks.

"Well, I wouldn't listen, you see. Your father kept trying to tell me that Aunt Grace was his sister, but I didn't want to hear him say he was in love with her. I knew it would hurt too much to hear him say it, so I allowed myself to think the worst. I let my emotions rule my head."

Rachel searches her daughter's face, for any clues that her words have hit a nerve. She can't tell for certain, but she thinks she saw a glimmer of recognition at her last words.

"Of course, when I finally decided to confront my fears, instead of trying to avoid them, I found I had had nothing at all to worry about in the first place."

"Well, I'm so glad you did, otherwise I wouldn't be here," Libby replies, offering a slightly cheeky smile. She looks down at the table and draws a circle with her finger, then looks back up to her mother. "Why are you telling me this Mum?"

Rachel now knows she needs to be more direct.

"I want you to ask yourself darling, if you are running away from something without knowing the truth. Just, find out for sure…before you make any final decisions."

Libby is now certain her mother knows about Jim? But, of course, her grandmother would have noticed things at the story-telling. She may be getting old, but she is still as astute as ever. Her grandmother, aunt and mother are very close to each other, and as they were all at Barons Reach, they would have spent lots of time talking together. Libby knew they talked about her because they all cared, and especially because she was also their only granddaughter, niece and daughter.

Although she's pretty sure she already knows the truth, about Jim and Hanna, she has missed being at Barons Reach this weekend. She has been stewing about it. Why should she feel she has to stay away? She hasn't said anything to Jim to show him how she really feels. And she could easily have been visiting someone else in the workmen's area that day, and made an honest mistake. Thank goodness she hadn't told Hanna she was looking for Jim at the time. Teagan seems to think that Jim only had eyes for her, but she was probably just influenced by her desire to see her friend find a boyfriend. It would be a bit hard having a boyfriend in a different town, hundreds of kilometres away, so there really wouldn't be much point to it anyway. But, she had really missed going to Barons Reach and doing the story-telling this weekend. She had missed walking over the grassy hills and beside the sparkling river. She still loved the walking track at Binda, but it seemed more and more to be like a first love – a cherished memory. But - Barons Reach, was calling her! She was like a new love, yearning and full of longing; waiting for her. Perhaps she had confused those feelings for Barons Reach, with Jim. She had to go back to her....

"Do you think Aunt Grace and Grandma will want me back, after the way I cancelled on them," she asks her mother, with trepidation.

Rachel sighs deeply and smiles.

"Yes darling. I'm sure of it. Aunt Grace actually asked me to tell you that after next weekend, there are two weekends of tours in a row. It's busier than usual at the moment, and if you'd like to, she would love you to help out. And, Grandma Mary said she needs you to come back and do the story-telling."

"Did you do the story-telling?" Libby asks her mother.

"No. I offered, but your grandmother said that you are the only one who tells them properly," her mother replies with a grin.

"Oh Grandma," Libby says, returning her mother's grin. She leaves the table and begins making her mother's cup of tea, and a hot milo for herself. "Good," she adds, firmly, thinking about what her aunt and grandmother relayed to her via her mother. "I've been thinking a lot this weekend. I've decided to take a week or so, of annual leave. Stay at Barons Reach for a while, between the tour visits."

CHAPTER 13

Libby has just finished the last dreaming story for the night. Though she didn't want to admit it, she had hoped her grandmother would ask her to tell all of them again. But this time, she was torn between feeling happy and a little sad.

Her grandmother had loved telling the dreaming stories. She had taught them to her children and grandchildren, and narrated them to hundreds, if not thousands, of children, from far and wide. Libby will never forget the joy on the children's faces, the first time she had been at the fire-site when her grandmother told the dreaming stories. It had been so obvious, by the look on her face afterwards, that it gave her immense satisfaction, and – great pride.

So, Libby knew that the more her grandmother handed over the story-telling to her, the more it meant that her grandmother was not *able* to do it. Her grandmother's natural enthusiasm seemed to be declining, and it seemed to be because she was becoming a little breathless by continual talking, and sometimes she seemed to go off into a world of her own, as if she were talking to herself. At those times, Libby would notice some of the visitors leaning forward, as if straining to hear her. Therefore, it now also saddened her a little when she was asked to take over, or narrate all the dreaming stories.

Jim and Hanna are both here tonight, as she expected. She had noticed them standing at the back again. She wished she could stop sneaking a look now and then at them. There was no point. And she reminded herself, she still hadn't worked out if she really should like Jim anymore anyway. There was still that question mark about the scar on his face. It seemed to bother her more than she understood why. But, so what if he had been in a fight? It also had nothing to do with her, and she can't imagine Aunt Grace putting up with anyone who was a regular trouble maker, anyway, even if he were a good worker. She just can't imagine Jim being like that though, even if she hadn't seen him for ten years. It could have just been a one-off, and he may not have even started it. So, she really must put it out of her mind.

She turns to her grandmother and notices she has been watching her, and she is smiling from ear-to-ear.

"That my granddaughter. You make me so proud."

"Oh Grandma," she replies, touching her arm and rubbing it tenderly.

"Ah, here comes Jim," she says, although she is still looking at Libby.

Libby looks around her chair, expecting him to be somewhere behind her, but no-one is there. She looks back at her grandmother, frowning from confusion.

"Over there," her grandmother says, indicating the far side of the fire with her head.

Libby looks over where she has indicated, and sure enough, Jim is making his way around to them. She glances back at her grandmother, wondering how she knew he was coming, when she hadn't taken her eyes away from Libby. Her grandmother never ceased to surprise her.

Libby is watching Jim coming closer, but then he stops and looks behind him. Hanna is trailing him. It looks like she is following him, and called his name. They exchange a few words and Jim looks about to turn and continue walking around the fire-site, but before he does, Hanna stumbles and falls. He goes over to her and helps her up, but she doesn't seem to be able to put any weight on one of her legs. Surely she couldn't have twisted her ankle just from that, Libby thinks. But, it looks like she has. Jim seems to sense Libby watching him. He turns his head and looks at her.

"You best go over and see if they need help, hey? Her grandmother says. Libby hadn't been aware that her grandmother was watching the event unfold also.

"Why? It looks like Jim has it all under control," she replies, with retrained emotion.

"Well, it would be polite, granddaughter."

Libby can't argue with her grandmother about that, so she admonishes herself for her bad manners, and walks off quickly. As she reaches them, Hanna had found the perfect prop - Jim's shoulder. Libby notices a smirk on her face as their eyes meet.

Libby looks at Jim. "Is everything alright?" she asks, bluntly.

Jim looks uncomfortable, though Libby can't understand why. Perhaps he's just embarrassed that his girlfriend has two left feet, Libby surmises.

"Hanna may have a twisted ankle," he says, looking a bit dejected.

"If not worse," Hanna says, looking up at Jim with a pained expression.

Jim sighs. "Well, I guess I better drive you home then."

Hanna smiles up gratefully at Jim, and turns to face Libby, a look of triumph on her face.

"Well, it seems like you have everything under control. Goodnight," Libby says, and turns to walk back around to her grandmother. She'll be damned if she has any intention of telling her she hopes it feels better soon. *I won't allow her to make me into a liar.* But she only manages two steps before Hanna says loudly, "I think you better carry me Jim."

No Libby, don't turn around. Don't give her that satisfaction, she commands herself. And she didn't. She decides that even if Hanna already has Jim for a lover, she has certainly made it clear that no other woman can come near him. Well, if that's the way it's going to be, so be it!

'What's going on 'round there," Grandma Mary asks when she arrives back.

"Oh nothing Jim can't handle, I'm sure," she says as she folds up her camp seat. "Are you ready Grandma?" she asks curtly.

"Well, looks like I got no choice in the matter now, does it granddaughter?" she replies grumpily, but the twinkle in her eye gives her away. "Hey, it be alright child. You see," she adds, with a wide smile, and lets Libby help her to stand.

***

Libby waves goodbye to her mother and grandmother, as they drive away from Murruway. She watches the car weave its way around the corner of the garden, and disappear from view. She turns and makes her way back inside.

Her mother had insisted on coming to collect her grandmother. She said there was no need for Libby to bring her home after the weekend, or come back to collect her for the following weekend. She would do it. Libby protested, not wanting her mother to have to make so many trips, but her mother insisted. Libby knew there was no point in arguing.

Aunt Grace was busy attending to the laundry from her grandmother's visit. Libby offered to take care of it, but Aunt Grace insisted she was fine with it, and suggested Libby might like to go for a walk, as it was such a nice day. She paused as she put the sheets in the washing machine and looked at Libby, obviously thinking.

"I wonder if you'd mind doing me a favour though, if you're going for a walk. Are you going in any particular direction?"

"No, I haven't decided yet, so of course, Aunt Grace. What would you like me to do?"

"Well, I believe Hanna has the keys to the stores shed. I asked the Manager to give them to her to get some things they need for the house. I want to make a duplicate set when I go into town in the morning. I don't want to call and disturb her on a Sunday. She would feel obligated to bring them over."

Libby feels like time has stopped. She can't seem to find her voice.

"But, it's ok if you don't want to walk in that direction. I can drive over later and collect them," Grace says, noticing her niece's hesitation.

"No, it's fine Aunt Grace. No problem. I'll head over there now," she replies, finally finding her voice.

***.

Of all the people at Barons Reach, it would have to be Hanna she asked her to see. Libby leaves the garden still shaking her head about it.

Well, it didn't really matter of course. She would just go up to the door, knock and politely ask for the keys. If Jim answered instead, she would just do exactly the same. Simple!

That decided, she begins to relax and take more notice of her surroundings, as she walks along the track that leads to the workmen's houses.

She can feel the warmth all around her on this beautiful spring day. Even in the rich brown soil, beneath her feet, interrupted only by snatches of stumpy grass and yellow daisies.

At Binda and Jannali, there is only one track between the two houses. It is close to the river and thick with scrub, as well as trees.

This track is only one of several on Barons Reach, but it couldn't be more different to the one at Binda and Jannali.

This track is in a clearing, so there are no surprises from dense scrub along the way. It is easy to see a kangaroo or snake approaching and hard to startle a cockatoo or parrot. Any bird can clearly see any movement from the trees far away, or above, from the sky. Therefore, she doesn't pose a threat to any magpies, yet unfamiliar with her face, and she is safe from being pecked by their sharp beaks, as they earnestly protect their nests. It is easy for her to let her mind wander as she walks along this track.

The land at Barons Reach is comprised of rolling hills and valleys, with only a smattering of trees, here and there, except for nearer to the river. In many ways, the threes and scrubland around the river here is very similar to that of Binda and Jannali, although not as dense. She likes the fact that the same river runs through all three properties, even though Barons Reach is so far away from Binda and Jannali.

The emerald green grassland is dotted with sheep, thousands and thousands of sheep. She often hears them bleating on still summer nights, when the windows are open where she sleeps, just like she does at Binda. It is like a lullaby, soothing, comforting.

Looking over at some trees, Libby thinks about their cubby house, and decides she will visit it soon, well, where it used to be, anyway. She wonders if she will find any part of it still there. She doubts it, after all these years, but she will still be able to imagine it none-the-less. She smiles as she remembers some of the things they did together, back then; all those years ago.

The workmen's houses are coming into view now. She heads towards the one where she knows Hanna lives. She begins to slow her steps, aware only now that she has been striding purposefully along. The walk has relaxed her, although she would never have imagined it possible when she first set out for her destination.

There is no need to be anxious though. No one knows how she had been feeling these last few weeks - especially and most importantly, Jim. She has nothing to feel embarrassed or ashamed of.

All of a sudden, she has arrived at her destination. She takes a big breath, and knocks – loudly, at the front door. She has no intention of dilly-dallying. She wants to get this, over and done with.

The door opens and Hanna stands in front of her. She doesn't look at all surprised. Libby imagines she must have looked out the window to see who was at the door, before answering.

"Hi, I'm here to collect the keys to the stores shed, for Aunt Grace. She asked me to come and collect them."

There, she has made it clear why she is there. Now all she needs is for Hanna to go get them, hand them to her, and she can be off.

"Alright then. I'll just go and get them," Hanna replies abruptly, turns and walks off quickly.

In no time at all, she is back, handing her the keys.

"Thank you Hanna," Libby says, attempting to maintain her manners, though she is finding it very difficult. She really doesn't like being around Hanna, at all.

It has nothing at all to do with Jim, she tells herself. It's just that she has never liked people who manipulate others to get what they want, or in this case, keep what is theirs. She can't imagine why Jim puts up with it. It is obvious to Libby. Surely that type of behaviour shouldn't be necessary in a relationship.

Well, she reminds herself, it is still none of her business, so she should just keep a watch on her own behaviour. She has always greatly disliked bad manners, or cattiness, as some woman have a tendency to be. She needs to remain mindful of herself in that regard, when she is dealing with Hanna. This woman just seems to be determined to get under her skin. And despite her thoughts on the matter, as she turns to leave, she stops and says with a forced smile, "I see your leg has healed. Remarkable recovery."

She is almost at the garden gate, when she hears Hanna respond, "Yes, well Jim knows how to take care of a woman."

Libby pretends not to hear, and it takes all her self-will not to slam the garden gate shut. She shouldn't have said what she said, and especially the way she said it - sinking to Hanna's level. If she could kick herself right now, she would. Several times. She takes off, retracing her steps, and by the time she arrives back at Murruway, she is almost breathless from having half-run the entire way. She had been so angry at herself. Hanna had every right to say what she had said. Once again, she had no one to blame but herself. Well, surely she won't have to go near Hanna again. She just realises, she didn't see Jim while she was there. Well, he could be doing anything on a Sunday. Who knows, or cares, she pretends to herself.

CHAPTER 14

Libby went into Bathurst with her aunt the next day. She followed her around as she took care of some business, stopping at the local hardware store to cut the stores shed keys, and to Office Works, to purchase some stationary supplies for her office.

However, while her aunt attended an appointment with her Accountant, she opted to walk around the big park close by, instead. Aunt Grace found her about an hour later.

"Do you know, this is the park your grandmother and I visited the day I found out I had been left Baron's Reach?" Grace says, as they sit on the park seat, overlooking the pond where ducks paddled gracefully through the water. "I wasn't much older than you at that time," she adds.

"It must have been a huge surprise," Libby says, smiling at her aunt.

"Oh yes, there were quite a few surprises that day," Grace replies, nodding.

"How did you meet Uncle Dan?" Libby asks.

"At tennis! Your mother and I were sharing a unit, or flat, as we called them back then..."

"Oh, I remember Mum telling me that now," Libby interjects.

Grace nods and continues, "…well, your mother and I were playing in the annual spring comp, in Dubbo. It was a mixed comp. We had to partner with a male. Your mother partnered your father. It was before they were married. I partnered with one of our friends – Johno, Uncle Dan's younger brother." She pauses and watches Libby put the pieces together. "Well, the moment I met Uncle Dan, I was well and truly smitten. I don't know what you'd call it these days, but that's how I felt," she says, smiling, and her eyes twinkle.

Libby thinks it is so lovely to hear her aunt tell her such a personal story, and to see her happiness in the memory.

"Smitten, sounds good to me. I might even make it my new favourite word," she replies, grinning at her aunt.

Aunt Grace returns a grin, but then she turns back to looking at the pond, and sighs.

"You know, it wasn't all that straight-forward though."

Libby was also looking at the pond, and she thought her aunt was talking to herself at first, but then she turned her head and glanced at her.

"When I first met your Uncle Dan at tennis, he was partnered with a woman he had known nearly all his life. She was chasing him."

Libby catches her breath, and Grace notices, but she remains looking at the pond. She continues…

"She even tried to get me out of the picture by trying to make me feel ashamed of being part Wiradjuri."

Libby doesn't make any movement or sound, but Grace is aware she is listening intently.

"I nearly let her win!" she says, now turning to Libby, who is looking at her with dismay.

"But, Aunt Grace, you of all people would never be ashamed of your Wiradjuri side. It doesn't make sense. Just look at all you've done at Barons Reach," she says, with conviction.

Grace pats her leg, to reassure her.

"Yes, but this was before I inherited Barons Reach. And also, it wasn't Barons Reach that rectified my way of thinking. It was your grandmother," she says with a soft smile.

Libby nods, knowing no response to that last statement is needed. Grandma Mary was the backbone of the family. The one person, who always seemed to know more about anyone in her family, than even they did, themselves. She was an enigma.

"But,…" Grace looks at her as if what she is about to say is very important. "if she hadn't told me to stop *running*, I would never have ended up with Uncle Dan."

Libby just realises that this is the second conversation she has had recently which has focused on – running; first her mother, now her aunt. They both said they had almost lost their true loves, because they had been running from the truth. And it had applied not only to love for her father, in her mother's case, and Uncle Dan, in her aunt's, but to their homes, their heritage. Both their love for the men in their lives, had also been linked with their love of the land, and in her aunt's case, both land and heritage were the same. There was no doubt in her mind that somehow there was meaning behind their words, intended for her. But – what was it?

Well, yes, she had run away from Barons Reach when she was ten years old. But she had only been a child then, and besides, she had had good reason, hadn't she?

Perhaps she had, in regard to Roger. She had been frightened of him. Any child in her shoes would have been. Then she suddenly realises something she had never considered before. Jim had only been a child himself, and if Roger had frightened her, of course he would have also felt threatened, especially when he had had to stay. Oh, how he must have felt – trapped. Why hadn't she seen that before? What kind of friend had she been to him anyway? She had called him her best friend, and look what *she* had done. She had deserted him!

Nevertheless, she doesn't really think that that is the message she is supposed to be hearing. However, any further thoughts on the matter swiftly come to an end, when her aunt makes a move to leave the park and return to Barons Reach. Libby feels there is much more she needs to consider. It is as if a door is slowly opening in her mind.

CHAPTER 15

The following day, Libby decided it was time to revisit all the places and events of her childhood at Barons Reach. She felt she needed to walk down memory lane, however sad it may be.

Her first stop was the little grave in the corner of the garden. Although she first came back for the tours over a month ago, she has not yet visited Tiger's grave. It was now only a mound of soft lawn, but the little cross she had made from two sticks, remained. She was surprised to see it still there, after all these years.

"You were an amazing little dog Tiger. I loved you so much. Thank you for the time we had together," she says softly, but instead of being brought to tears, as she thought she would, she smiles gently, remembering. "You sure liked to be in the thick of things though, didn't you? You were so brave."

As she walks out the garden and heads for the river, she thinks about the words she just spoke at Tiger's grave. He never ran away from anything, always approached things head on. Being brave, no doubt, is what brought about his death, but he would have died fighting. She was proud of him.

She now sits on the grassy riverbank, resting her arms on bended knees, looking into the water.

She remembers the times she and Jim had been here together, swimming and splashing each other on hot summer days. The current had been so strong. It had been hard to keep from floating downstream. Jim had been a much stronger swimmer though. One day, the river almost got the better of her. She had yelled out to Jim, just before the force of the river had pulled her under. She hadn't known if he had heard her. But, either he had heard her, or he had been watching her, because he suddenly appeared out of nowhere, held on to her, and pulled her to the bank.

The day Roger had followed them here, she shouldn't have been afraid. Roger had tried to push Jim into the river, but even if he had, Jim would have been ok. And even if Roger had pushed *her* in, she has no doubt now, that Jim would have rescued her, like he had before. She imagines Jim would even have been a better swimmer than Roger too, even though he had been four years younger. Jim knew the river so well, just like he knew every track of Barons Reach. He has lived here since he was five-years-old, after all.

One day they built a makeshift boat, from twigs they found nearby. They tied it together with the stringy part of the leaves from a eucalyptus tree. They knew the river ran all the way down past Binda and Jannali, hundreds of kilometres away, but they had faith that the little boat would float right past there. They tried to work out how fast the river ran, and convert it to distance, but neither of them had a clue how to do it, so they just decided to give it a go. Libby promised she would look out for it when she returned to Binda. She actually did go to the river the day she returned to Binda, anticipating the little boat to float by. Of course, she didn't see it, and it had probably fallen apart the moment they had lost sight of it. But it had been so much fun.

She thinks back to the dream she had at the unit recently, where had been trying to swim upstream, to Barons Reach, and Jim. It had been so vivid. Seeing Roger beneath the water had shaken her for quite a while afterwards. But, in her dream, he hadn't hurt her, or been able to. He had been buried beneath the water. Drowned. Perhaps her dream had been telling her that he was no longer a part of Barons Reach. That he couldn't hurt her anymore.

She suddenly realises she doesn't know what happened to Roger. How long he had stayed at Barons Reach, or even if he has actually left. She has just assumed he has, because she hasn't seen him. That doesn't mean he is no longer still here though. She must ask Aunt Grace, she decides.

As for the water pulling her back, in her dream, well, she had read somewhere that dreaming about water, referred to – emotions. That, calm water meant feeling peaceful, and choppy water meant feeling upset. Something like that. So, because the river had been so rough and strong, she thinks it probably meant that she had been battling with her emotions. That made sense at least. She saw the truth in it.

When she arrives at the cubby house, she cannot believe what she sees. It is still fully intact, almost exactly as she had last seen it. It couldn't possibly have remained like this without someone maintaining it, she thinks. She picks up one of the long sticks leaning against the outside of the roughly assembled building. It was very light, even lighter than she expected. How on earth could it have remained leaning against the structure like that all these years? All around, she can see branches and twigs that have been torn from the surrounding trees, by windstorms that have swept through the area. Someone has been maintaining it. She can't recall there being any other children on the property. Well, when she was last here, anyway. Jim had been the only child before Roger turned up. At the story-telling, all the children has been visitors. Could it have been Jim?

She can see she would no longer be able to squeeze through the front door. The structure would easily fall apart if she were to attempt it. So she moves to a tree close by, and leans back against its trunk, studying the tree above the cubby-house.

It looks different to how she remembers. She can't recall seeing that black hollowed out section, half way up, before. She wonders what had caused it. Perhaps a lightning strike? Grandma Mary had shown her a tree that had once been hit by lightning. It had survived, and continued to grow. Maybe that's what happened to this tree.

When she looks again at the cubby-house, she can see that it also looks slightly different, although she can't put her finger on it. Perhaps it's just that she is older, bigger, taller. Maybe she is just looking at it from a different perspective, because, overall, it still looks very much like the design of the original structure.

This was their favourite place on Barons Reach. So many adventures, and so many secrets and dreams were shared here. She closes her eyes and listens. She can hear the laughter of her childhood days with Jim, echoing through the trees, and as if on cue, a kookaburra laughs with joy, in the memory. She smiles to herself as the kookaburra's laugh reverberates above her.

Jim told her, in secret, that he wanted to be the Property Manager of Barons Reach one day, like Bill Sutton. He said he would make sure that all the workers were treated right too, like Bill Sutton did. Libby told him she was sure he would be a good Property Manager.

She told him, in secret, that she wanted to live in a big house one day, like the one at Barons Reach. She said that way, she would never get bored of where she lived, because it would take forever to explore each room. Jim said he thought that was pretty alright, and asked if he could visit. Libby said she would like that, because it wouldn't be as much fun exploring without him.

She remembers now that they had high-fived each other then. In a way, it had been – a pact. They had been so close in those days.

Had he really changed, or was she imagining it? Even if he hasn't though, she can only ever consider him as a friend now, because of Hanna.

But, she had her childhood memories, and that was something no one could take away from her; something she could keep, forever.

CHAPTER 16

"I'm wondering Libby dear, if you'd be interested in having more of a look around. I mean, I think you've really only seen the parts of Barons Reach closest to the house. Are you interested in seeing more?"

Libby has been lying on one of the sofas in the library, next door to Aunt Grace's office. She hadn't seen her aunt enter the room, because she had been so absorbed in the little red book in her hands, with its tiny font. It was very old, and she knew it was a famous classic, although she has not yet read it: 'Jane Eyre' by Charlotte Bronte.

The library has so many classics, and books she has never heard of too. If only she could take the entire library, intact, and somehow move it to her unit. Of course, it wouldn't fit there. Then again, she could always borrow the books, but she likes reading them here, in the library at Barons Reach, so she would just have to make the most of it when she was here.

"That would be lovely, Aunt Grace," she responds putting the book she was holding up, down on her lap. "When would you like to do it?"

"Well, the thing is, I have to finish up some paperwork before my appointment with my solicitor, tomorrow afternoon. Then, we only have two days before the next tour, and I think you said you'll be going back to Dubbo, after that. You know you are more than welcome to stay as long as you like dearest," she ends, but as if it were a question, and not a statement.

"Thank you Aunt Grace," she replies, smiling. "I love being here. In fact, I wish I could stay a lot longer, but I have to go back for work..."

But, before Libby can finish what she was about to say, her aunt walks quickly into the room and sits on the edge of the sofa beside her.

"Do you really Libby? I mean...I want to ask you something, and it's quite important to me. I hope you won't just answer to please me. I really need to know... If Grandma and I weren't around, do you think you would still like to continue with the tours? Or even, keep an eye on Barons Reach, make sure Windradyne's gravesite and the house don't get damaged in any way?

Aunt Grace looks at her anxiously, and Libby does feel a bit put on the spot, and also - sad, at the thought of her grandmother and aunt not being around. But she looks around the library, and thinks about Murruway, Windradyne's gravesite, and Barons Reach, as a whole. She can't imagine not being here in the future - telling the stories around the fire, ensuring Windradyne's graveside and Mulluway remain as beautifully kept as they are. She looks affectionately at her aunt.

"Aunt Grace, I will never run away from Barons Reach again, and I will do all I can to make sure everything on Barons Reach is looked after," she answers with conviction.

Aunt Grace releases a big breath she has not been aware she has been holding in.

"Thank you dearest, that's all I needed to know," she says, patting Libby's leg. She stands and begins walking towards the door, but when she is almost there, she stops, and turns. "Oh, now about seeing more of the place. As I said, I'm a bit tied up myself, with things I now feel much better about, thanks to you…" she smiles, and continues, "…but, it's forecast to rain the day after tomorrow, and as I'm busy tomorrow, would you mind if I asked Jim to show you?"

Libby can't believe the opportunity she has just been presented with. She had decided she would talk to Jim at the story-telling on Friday night. After thinking about what her mother and aunt had said about running away from things, and after visiting all their old favourite places on Barons Reach, she has felt much clearer about her relationship with Jim. They had shared so much as children, and they had been best friends then, so why couldn't they at least be friends again? Jim's personal life was none of her business. And, although it happened a long time ago, she needs to apologise to him for not coming back after Tiger died. Aunt Grace's suggestion sounds like the perfect opportunity to do that.

"No, that will be fine Aunt Grace, thank you."

"Very good then. I'll ask him to pick you up here tomorrow morning. How about nine? Does that sound alright?"

"Yep, thank you," she replies, and as her aunt turns towards the door again Libby raises the book, scanning the page in an attempt to remember where she has last read to. But, she immediately drops it to her lap again. She looks over and sees that Aunt Grace is almost through the door.

"Aunt Grace, before you go…"

She waits for her aunt to turn again.

"I've been meaning to ask…what happened to Roger?"

Grace's face drops a little, and Libby notices, as well as the way she is hesitating with her answer.

"Well…" her aunt begins, obviously weighing up her words. "I think that's something you should perhaps ask Jim," she replies, and she turns quickly and disappears into the hallway, before Libby can say anything else.

Libby is dumbfounded by her aunt's reply. Why should she ask Jim? Aunt Grace knew everything about Barons Reach, after all. Why couldn't she tell her? She thinks it is very strange, but it looks like she has no choice. She will just have to ask Jim.

.

CHAPTER 17

Jim returns the cordless phone to its cradle. He walks out to the verandah, sits on the top step, places his elbows on his knees and rests his chin in his cupped hands.

Just what he doesn't need, he thinks – about three hours alone with Libby. That's about how long it will take him to show her a good section of Barons Reach.

He knew Barons Reach like the back of his hand now. He and his father have lived here for over fifteen years. Not as long as Bill Sutton, though, the former Property Manager.

His father has been Property Manager for just on ten years now. Grace offered him the position as soon as Bill had handed in his resignation. They had all been a bit sad that Bill had left the way he did.

Jim's father kept in touch with him. He told Jim that Bill had found a nice little place of his own, on the other side of Bathurst. Nothing very big, but big enough for him to handle on his own, a few sheep, and a little creek running through it. He said he was content. That had made everyone, especially Grace, relieved.

He got on well with Grace. She refused to let him call her Mrs Matthews. She said he was to call her Grace, that he was like family to her, and she couldn't abide him calling her anything else.

He hadn't known what Barons Reach had been like under the old owner, but he'd heard she had been very set in her ways. A bit of a dragon, some had said, very *old school*. He was glad he and his father had come after Grace took over.

He liked all her family. Mary was a character, that was for sure. And what she did for the visitors was amazing. His father said that because of Grace and Mary, Barons Reach changed from being owned solely by a long line of white people, to being shared by thousands of people, both white and aboriginal. Grace and Mary had given back.

His father didn't have any aboriginal ancestry, but he had married an aboriginal woman, part Wiradjuri - his mother. He had only been five when she died. He remembers very little of his first five years, but he can never forget the last time he saw her in that hospital bed; her beautiful warm and soft creamy skin, against the cold, stiff white hospital sheets. His father had lifted him up to let her kiss him, as she struggled to raise her arms to hug him, one last time. That's the last memory he has of her. He used to take his treasure box, as he used to call it, out of the cupboard every year when it was her birthday. He would go through the contents and try to remember. But, he hasn't done that for years, and sometimes now, he finds it hard to even remember what she looked like. Unless he looks at a photgraph.

He hadn't forgotten what Libby looked like though. He can still see her as she was when they were ten. He remembers that dog too; Tiger. Brave little thing. What he did with that roo, especially. He hates to think past that, because that was when Roger came, and Libby left. He had missed her so much.

Now she was almost twenty-one, and she was so beautiful. He nearly couldn't speak when he saw her again that first time, at the story-telling. She took his breath away. She was sitting next to Mary, and she looked like one of those lead actors in a movie, he thought at the time. She would be certain to have a boyfriend back in Dubbo. He felt like he was in a dream when she told the dreaming stories. Her voice was so soothing and mellow, but clear enough to hear, even where he stood at the back. But, she also made it clear, when he spoke to her, that she didn't want to spend much time talking to him. Left pretty quickly after the story-telling. And that last night, when Hanna fell over. Well, he could tell she didn't really care about either of them. He had been really surprised by that. She had always been so caring as a child, so sympathetic about any bird or animal's plight. Where had that gone? Well, it wasn't his business, anyway. She was the owner's niece, and he just had to do what he was told to do.

He stands up and walks back into the house. He'd better get tea ready. It is his turn. His father will be wondering where it is, soon.

**

Libby takes one more look at herself in the long mirror in the centre of the wardrobe. She decided on jeans and a silky blue top that matches her sky-blue eyes. It was going to be a warm day, but she would take her light beige jacket, just in case. She wasn't one for jewellery at the best of times, but she added a little heart-shaped silver pendant Aunt Grace had given her for her tenth birthday. It seemed appropriate, somehow. For once, her hair seemed to be co-operating. Teagan would be pleased.

She knocks on the open door to the library, and when Aunt Grace looks up, she says, "I'm going out the front to wait now."

"Ok dear. Have a nice time," her aunt replies, smiles, and returns her gaze to her computer.

Libby closes the garden gate and leans back against it. She tries to still her nerves.

A Holden ute comes into view, and she inhales a big breath and expels it. Jim alights, after the ute stops.

"Hello," he says smiling, walks around to the passenger door, and opens it for her.

"Hi," she replies, with a smile as well, and seats herself in the ute.

"So, I'm taking you for a bit of a tour of Barons Reach today," he says, as they drive away from Murruway.

"Yes, thank you for doing this," she says, glancing at him.

"No problem. I'll take you past some of the buildings and the old shearing shed, and then north to one of the newer shearing sheds, if you like. Does that sound ok?" he asks, glancing at her.

"Yep. Sounds good."

"Are you up to opening and closing a few gates though?" he asks. "Be quicker that way," he adds.

"Yes, of course," she replies. So, she thinks, he wants to get this over and done with as soon as possible. Well, she will just make sure she takes in as much as she can. She has been looking forward to seeing more of Barons Reach, ever since her aunt made the suggestion. That Jim was taking her was just a bonus. She could kill two birds with one stone. But, she would wait a bit first. She wasn't sure how he would react now to an apology that was so long overdue. He might feel uncomfortable about it, or he might just shrug it off. Either way, she would feel uncomfortable with that too. No, she must wait for the right time.

As he said, they soon drove past several building, and he explained what each one was.

There was the stores shed, which looked nothing like a shed. It was made of sandstone and although it had aged with time, looked like it would last for another hundred years or so. Jim said that in olden times, it had stocked provisions for the house and the workers, but these days, it just stocked provisions for the visitor cabins and some household things for the workers.

Close by the stores shed, there were several newer machinery sheds, made of galvanised iron, and then they came to the old shearing shed and the horse stables. Both these were built of the same sandstone as the stores shed, and they were huge. Jim said they had both been built in olden times, when the Bartlett's didn't own as much land and they used horses.

Libby says, wistfully, without thinking. "We could have had so much fun exploring the shearing shed and stables."

Then realising what she had said, she glances at Jim.

With his eyes still on the road, he says, "Yeah, I reckon. We just weren't allowed up this way, remember?" Then he glances at her and catches her eyes.

"Well, we had enough to keep us occupied on the other side, anyway," she says, turning to look out her side window.

They continue along the road, heading away from the buildings, but he points towards his side window. "The workmen's houses are down that way, from here. You'd remember that no doubt."

"Ahum, they haven't changed much," she replies. She then thinks that may have sounded a bit rude, so she adds. "Well mostly. The garden looks lovely around your house though. Hanna's done a great job with it."

Jim looks thoughtful. She must have been there sometime recently.

"Yep, they've made it look a lot better than it used to when Dad and I lived there."

Libby frowns and turns to him.

"But, don't you live there?

He turns to her, also frowning.

"No, Dad and I live in the Manager's house. Didn't you know? Dad's been the new Property Manager ever since…well, for about ten years now."

Libby frown dissolves and she is clearly surprised.

"No, I didn't know. I thought you lived with …Hanna."

Jim chuckles. "No, no way," he says, with a big grin. "That girl is a handful. I try to stay as far away as possible from her. Not all that easy when you live so close though," he adds.

Libby is torn between being mad at Hanna for deceiving her, or happy that Jim isn't living with her. He could still have a girlfriend though, who lives somewhere else. And, had Hanna really done anything wrong, except try to win Jim, and eliminate any obstacles?

Libby smiles to herself, and she feels like a weight has been lifted, but she still won't go past the friendship line. Ten years is a long time. She has no idea what has happened in his life during that time.

"Well, congrats to your Dad. I think that's wonderful. So, you're officially, the Manager's son, then," she says, attempting to lighten the mood.

It seems to have had the opposite effect on Jim, because his smile disappears and he adds, "And you are still the owner's niece," as he returns to watch the road ahead.

CHAPTER 18

After Jim dropped her off at the house, Libby went into the kitchen to prepare lunch. Aunt Grace walked in as she opened the fridge.

"Hello dear. How was your tour?" she asks, with expectant eyes.

"It was good, thank you," she replies, and puts her head in the fridge to collect some salad ingredients and some sliced chicken meat. She turns briefly to look at her aunt standing near the door. "Have you had lunch yet?" she asks.

"Yes. I've already eaten, and I'd better get myself into town for my appointment now. Is there anything you'd like me to get you while I'm in Bathurst?" she asks.

"No thanks. I'm all good," she says, with a smile.

"Ok then. I'll be back later this arvo," she says, looking curiously at Libby as she walks out of the kitchen.

Libby is glad she has some time alone now, even though she doesn't see all that much of her aunt during the day. Aunt Grace has ensured she spends time with Libby during the evenings though, while she has been here alone with her. They either watch TV or read together, in the lounge room. Sometimes they play cards. Aunt Grace said they played cards a lot of when she was younger. Libby decided that was probably why she won most of the time.

Libby forgets sometimes that Aunt Grace will be fifty soon, half a century. She doesn't think her aunt looks at all old though. She could easily pass for her late thirties still. Well, from a distance, anyway. She has never really noticed any wrinkles on her face, although she must have them. Sometimes she notices her hair is a little grey at the sides when she is due to colour it again, though. She is really quite beautiful, inside and out, and she couldn't have a nicer aunt.

She is glad she is all alone now because she wants to think about Jim, without the possibility of interruption. Relive the drive they just took together. It certainly revealed some truths, and she finally apologised to him.

That he wasn't living with Hanna had been a huge relief. She was surprised by how much it had affected her though. It wasn't as if knowing he wasn't living with Hanna, was the only obstacle to...to what, she thinks? Wasn't she only thinking of friendship now, she reminds herself? Well, she still had other things to find out. She hasn't asked about that scar, although, as she continually reminds herself, it is none of her business. Does it really matter, anyway? For some inexplicable reason though - it does! She will just have to ask him, she tells herself, so she can get it out of her mind. She also hadn't asked him about Roger, as her aunt had suggested, and it seems he is the only person she can ask to find out.

She had really enjoyed his company, although for a few minutes after he had mentioned that she was the niece of the owner, he had closed up. She can't understand why he had done that. After all, he has always known she was Aunt Grace's niece. As if she could change that!

She found that a bit odd.

However, aside from that, they had chatted amicably about the property, and he had shown her the newer galvanised iron, shearing shed, on the northern side. He had even teased her by pretending to drive off and leave her, when she had opened one of the gates. She had told him that unless he promised not to do that, she wouldn't open any more. So he promised, and he behaved after that. It had been fun though.

Finally, when he pulled up outside Murruway, she had thanked him for showing her more of the property, and then she said…

"Jim, there's something I've been meaning to say to you. I should have said it a lot sooner, but…well…I guess I should apologise for that….too. Anyway…I want to apologise, for not coming back, after…when I was ten."

Until this moment, she had been glancing away from his eyes as she spoke. She had been trying to keep looking at him, but he was looking into her eyes so intently, it was distracting her. However, right now, she needs him to see the truth of her words, in her eyes, so she maintains contact.

"We were best friends. I let you down, and I am so very sorry Jim. I hope you can forgive me."

Her eyes misted over with tears as she spoke the last few words. He remained looking at her throughout her apology, and now she is looking into his eyes, he reaches over and cups her cheek in his warm hand, so softly, she almost melts into it.

"There's no need to apologise Libby. It was a really tough time for you, with what happened to Tiger and...I understood why you didn't come back. But, I missed you...very much."

He remained looking into her eyes, as he took his hand away. It broke the spell, and they both looked away.

"Well, thank you," she said softly, as she alighted from the car.

"No problem," he replied, with a catch in his voice, and once she closed the door, he quickly drove off around the corner.

Libby decides she can't eat just yet, so she replaces the food items back in the fridge and retreats to the verandah, to admire the view.

That touch didn't feel like a friend's touch. The way he was looking at her, didn't look the way a friend would look. And she really liked – both!

She still needs to ask him about Roger and the scar, but she was afraid, she now admits, but more afraid to find out that she won't like the answers.

Her mother had recently told her that she had been afraid of the truth, and nearly lost her father. Right now, she knows that if she doesn't ask him, she won't be able to move forward with him in any type of relationship, anyway. *If,* it were to go that way. So what was the difference, even if his answers were not what she hoped to hear?

***

The next day, Libby awoke to a cloudy sky, and it looked like her aunt had been right; rain was coming. As she looked further out, she could see darker clouds. A summer storm.

After breakfast, she walked up the wooden staircase to the top section of the house, along the long corridors and into each room. The echo of her footsteps the only sound breaking the silence.

This is only the third time she has been up here since she was a child.

The first time was when she had recently conducted the tour for Aunt Grace. At that time, however, she had been focussed on reading all the information to the visitors, and answering any questions.

The visiting adults had been genuinely impressed by the grandness of the upstairs of the house, and they had warned their children to either, hold their hand, not touch anything, or at the least – behave.

Libby had hidden a little smile when she had first heard an adult reprimanding a child for running along the corridor. She understood that the adult was only showing respect, but when she had been little, she had run up and down the very same corridors with wild abandon, sometimes even using the timber floors in her socks to test her sliding skills. She hadn't intended to be disrespectful. She had just felt comfortable in every part of Murruway.

The second time she had recently been here, had been with Teagan. It had felt really good to show her friend a part of her life from her childhood. But, as usual, Teagan had hardly stopped talking as she had taken her from room to room.

She is able to listen to the silence now, and yet she is sure she can hear whispering all around her. It is almost as if she is being watched and discussed. She attempts to ignore those thoughts, but all of a sudden, she is almost convinced she just heard a child's laughter. It doesn't frighten her. It almost feels like Murruway is just showing her that there were once children who lived here too, that even before she skidded and shrieked with joy through the corridors, other children had also, long ago.

She walks into the main bedroom, which once belonged to Aunt Grace's grandmother, Mrs Bartlett. It is the grandest of all the bedrooms. Mrs Bartlett would have spent a lot of time here in her latter days, when she was too frail to take the stairs as much as she normally would. She must have been quite fit in her younger days though. The stairs were quite a height, and even Libby found she needed to catch her breath once she made it to the top.

She imagines Mrs Bartlett would have read quite a lot in bed. The library downstairs was testament to that. Perhaps, when her eyes become blurred from reading, she had looked out the huge window and marvelled at the scene before her. The gentle green rolling hills, dotted with sheep, and fluffy white clouds, interrupting a crystal-clear, blue sky.

Libby walks over to the window now, drawn by her thoughts. The foreboding storm still approaches in the distance. She envisions Mrs Bartlett, tucked up in bed, watching a lightning storm through this window. It would be majestic, perhaps a little frightening, but nevertheless, incredibly thrilling and fascinating.

She leaves the bedroom and walks along the corridor, and back down the stairs. She realises she is feeling nostalgic, but not for herself. It is almost as if she is carrying the memories of Murruway.

Mrs Bartlett must have been so lonely towards the end of her life, all alone in this big house. By that time, she had already lost her husband many years prior, and her only son had been killed in a car accident, only a few years before she passed. She would have had so much time to think about, reflect on, and deeply consider the one thing she was to leave behind, that had been so much a part of her life - Barons Reach.

As she walks past the office down stairs, Libby glances in at Aunt Grace. Her aunt is focused on some paperwork in front of her. She continues on, without disturbing her, knowing she has not even noticed her. She walks quietly out the front door, over to the garden side, half-wall, of the verandah, and leans against it, still deep in thought.

Mrs Bartlett had not been kind to her grandmother or aunt when they had been younger. She finds it difficult to understand how she could have taken Aunt Grace from her grandmother when she was a baby. However, she wonders, perhaps she didn't do it so much out of unkindness, but because she actually thought she was doing the right thing.

She had lived at a time when assimilation was the order of the day. It had been government policy at that time to take the aboriginals who had been fathered by white men, in an attempt to help them blend in with white society. There had later been those who disputed that theory, believing there had been other motivations behind it, namely to *breed out the colour* as it was said, because it was believed that eventually all full-blooded aboriginals would perish.

Most likely, she had not been aware of the ulterior motives, which had not been widely known at the time. Perhaps she really did believe Aunt Grace would have a much better life with a white Christian family. How could she have possibly let her granddaughter be taken by another family, if she had not felt she would have been well cared for? She may even have realised that Mary would not have been able to work and care for a baby as well. To think, that on that day that Aunt Grace was whisked away, Mrs Bartlett knew she was giving away the daughter of her only son; a granddaughter with Bartlett blood.

She had been a widow at that time. Her husband had passed away many years before. She only had a son and her respected name, left. What must have been going through her mind at that time? Was it pride, that had kept her from keeping the child, disgrace that her son had obviously bedded a part aboriginal woman? Or, was it as Libby hopes - that she did what she did, in the belief that it was the best thing for everyone.

Could it be, although Libby's grandmother would never in a million years agree, that at the end of her life, Mrs Bartlett had been given a small measure of reward, and some comfort, when her granddaughter unknowingly revealed her whereabouts to her. Perhaps Mrs Bartlett had wrestled greatly with her conscious in the days before she passed, regretted various actions she had taken, repented of the heartbreak she had caused, anguished over those things she could no longer change.

Libby looks up to the sky again. She still has time. She makes her way down the verandah steps and continues on, through the side garden gate. She feels as though she is being guided now, to Windradyne's gravesite.

As she strides purposefully towards her destination, Libby thinks about the reading Aunt Grace conducts at Windradyne' gravesite; the story about the Bathurst War, how the original Bartlett family established good relations with the Wiradjuri people, and the reason why the grave of Windradyne, the brave resistance leader and warrior, rests on Barons Reach.

Libby feels immense gratitude to the Bartlett family, for their kindness to Windradyne. She sometimes finds it difficult to comprehend the injustices enacted on the Wiradjuri people, and all Indigenous Australians, by white man, so she finds great relief in the knowledge that the early Bartlett family were not part of it.

One account she read, from the paperwork Aunt Grace had found in her grandmother's office, pertained to some close family members of Windradyne's, who had been murdered by some neighbouring farmers, at the height of the Bathurst War. Windradyne came to the Bartlett's door, seeking to serve justice to those responsible. James, the son of Charles Bartlett, the original settler of Barons Reach, happened to be at the house at the time. He was fluent in the Wiradjuri language, having learnt it through his interactions with Windradyne over the time he has already known him. He noticed the understandable unrest of the tribesmen with Windradyne, fitted out with all types of fighting weapons. He knew he could easily have become alarmed, but instead, he spoke calmly to Windradyne, reassuring him that his family were not guilty of such a transgression. Windradyne then spoke to the other members of his tribe who were with him. After a heated discussion, in which Windradyne spoke well of the Bartlett's, they were spared. However, not long after, those responsible for the deaths of his family members, were not so fortunate.

Libby finds it difficult to imagine how cruel many of the white settlers had been to the aboriginals in Australia. She is aware that the cruelty wasn't just inflicted on the Wiradjuri people of New South Wales, though. It applied to all aboriginals in Australia.

She has read somewhere that there were over two hundred and fifty aboriginal language groups in Australia, prior to white settlement, and each of those language groups had its own dreaming stories and way of life. However, after white settlement, and the eradication and displacement of so many aboriginals, it is difficult to even know how many of those language groups remain today.

It was true that the first pioneers saw the aboriginal people as being nomadic, moving around form place-to-place, therefore appearing – homeless. The white man did not see them lay any claim to land ownership. They did not understand that that was their way of life, and that it had in fact been their way of life for more than forty thousand years. And also, by living that way, they were respecting the land, caring for their natural resources, and allowing their food sources to be replenished in their short absences.

But, the white people kept coming, believing that the land was theirs for the taking, and killing any aboriginals in their way. What else could the aboriginals do, but everything they could, to protect their land and people. They – retaliated.

Libby recalls an account whereby some Wiradjuri people came upon a farmer who had successfully grown potatoes. As the farmer had actually already destroyed their main food source, through farming the land, they had been very hungry. Afraid of the dark-skinned people carrying their spears and other hunting tools, the farmer offered them some of his potatoes, hoping to appease them, so they would leave. The Wiradjuri people accepted the potatoes with gratitude. However, they returned a few days later and the farmer came across them helping themselves to the potatoes. Unbeknownst to the farmer, the Wiradjuri people had believed that as they had been shown the food, and it was on their land, it was considered natural that they could help themselves. The farmer did not like them helping themselves to what he considered to be his food, so the next time they visited, he offered them some bread, which had been poisoned. The Wiradjuri family accepted the gift and died. It was not surprising then, that the farmer was later killed by a Wiradjuri member, in retaliation.

Libby has read many accounts about the injustices dealt out to the Indigenous Australians, from the documents and diaries of Aunt Grace's ancestors. She understands however, that a great deal of what happened in the years after settlement, was due to ignorance, fear, and greed.

When she arrives at Windradyne's gravesite, the gentle breeze she had felt on her walk is now becoming quite strong. The wind whips her hair and her long summer dress clutches her legs.

However, she pays it no attention, as she stands in front of the grave and pays her respects.

The last time she has been here was when she had been ten. So long ago, and she apologises to Windradyne for her absence, before she begins her conversation.

"If only you could know Windradyne, how many people have come here to pay their respect to you. Not only people with Wiradjuri ancestors, but white people with no aboriginal ancestry, and people with ancestry from other aboriginal nations. I believe you would be pleased, but most of all, I believe you would be proud. And, I know you would be proud of Grandma Mary and Aunt Grace, for the work they are doing here at Barons Reach. You were right to trust the Bartlett's, because in the end, the last of the line handed this part of Wiradjuri country back to its people. Small comfort perhaps, considering the extent of the original size of Wiradjuri country, but there it is. I am so sorry that my white ancestors inflicted the atrocities that they did upon your people. I am so sorry they took away those things that were essential to your very existence, your land, your way of life, your spirituality. That they defiled your women, took away your children, and destroyed the land, which was always the fundamental reason of your being. They were ignorant, but that was no excuse. They were fearful, but that was no excuse. They were greedy, and that also, was no excuse.

But, you survived Windradyne. Your spirit lives on, here, at Barons Reach. It is in the rolling hills and secret valleys we explore as we walk, and in the green grass that tickles our bare feet. It is in the wind that brushes across our brow and cools our faces, and in the clear blue sky that darkens and pours rain upon our heads. It is in the cawing of the crow, the laughing of the kookaburra, the bleating of the sheep in pastures below. It is in the rocks on the highest hill, the river running wild and free, and in the sigh of the treetops above. And, it is also in -

the people, who *know*! Yes, you survived, Windradyne. Be at peace!"

As Libby finishes talking to Windradyne, she notices the wind is now so strong she has to fight it to remain still. She looks up at the sky, and at that moment a flash of lightning strikes in the distance, and the dark clouds she saw earlier, are now above her. Time to go!

She runs as fast as she can, wondering if she will make it back to Murruway before the heavens open up. She makes it to the top of the last hill, and she can see Murruway before her. Not far now, and although she knows she can waste no time, she hesitates as she looks upon the beauty of Barons Reach, all around her, in the stormy weather.

Another clap of thunder and she begins to run again, realising that she is enjoying it. It has been a long time since she has run. She feels invigorated, alive! She reaches the garden gate, and is just about to rejoice in having outrun the storm, when all of a sudden, rain falls down upon her, so heavily, that by the time she reaches the verandah, she is totally drenched.

She smiles as she shakes herself at the door. "Well, I almost had time," she says to herself, giggling.

CHAPTER 19

Libby sits before the fire, her grandmother on her right, and her mother, then Aunt Grace, on her left.

Her mother had brought her grandmother the previous evening, and she said she was staying until Sunday. She said it had been a long time since she had been at Barons Reach with her daughter, and she wanted to spend some time with *all* the girls, while they were together.

"Your father said he'll be working mainly at Jannali this weekend, so he will keep an eye on your grandfather, and he and Will are quite capable of feeding themselves, now and then. Besides, I want to listen to my daughter do the story-telling, at least - once," she said, to Libby.

Libby could not remember ever being completely alone with her mother, aunt and grandmother, together before. At family gatherings, birthdays and Christmas, at least one of the men, if not all of them, were there as well. So, Libby found the experience, in the least, very interesting.

She was fascinated by some of the stories they told, and she could see how they loved to relive the days when they were younger. Especially the part about when they had just found their true loves.

Even her grandmother joined in. Libby had never heard about how her grandmother had come to marry Grandpa Don. In fact, it was a bit of a shock to learn that she was originally his housekeeper, and that he had been married before. She also heard all about Viv, as her grandmother called her. She said her proper name was Vivien, and she had been her first real true friend.

"She was fully white too Libby, just like Grandpa. In those days, white people didn't think it was right to marry an aborigine, or even a part aborigine, and especially someone who was working for you. Your Grandpa though, he didn't care one iota, and he told me later that Viv even told him to marry me, the night she died." She then laughed, heartily, and Libby could not conceal the look of shock on her face. "No, granddaughter, it not like you think. That was Viv all over," she added. "She never mucked around when she reckoned she was right about something, and she was just lookin' out for your Grandpa. And it didn't matter to me she told him that, cause I could see when your Grandpa asked me to marry him later, he was lovin' me. Ya just know, don't ya?" she finished her narration, looking at Grace and Rachel. They both nodded and smiled as if they were both thinking about their own husbands too.

"Grandma, what happened to Viv?"

Mary had then suddenly lost her smile, and Libby immediately regretted her question.

"That demon, cancer, took her granddaughter. She so young, too. Only thirty. Cruel, it was. Downright, plain, cruel."

"Oh, I'm so sorry Grandma, I should never have asked."

Her grandmother had then looked almost horrified.

"No granddaughter, you need to ask these things. It good ta hear it from the horse's mouth, when you can, That way, it better chance of being the truth. You understand?"

"I guess," Libby had replied, looking uncertain.

"Well, that one reason we sharin' the dreaming stories, and all the things we know about the Wiradjuri people, to everyone, black and white. I know's they the truth, cause my family taught me, and now you tell them, the right way too. So, if we keep teach'n our kids the truth, no-one can take that away."

Libby had nodded. "Ok, Now, I understand. Thanks Grandma."

Mary had then looked at her granddaughter thoughtfully, and sighed deeply. "You want ta know the truth 'bout something, you got ta ask, granddaughter."

And once again, Mary's words had seemed to etch themselves in her mind, as she thought of Jim.

***

She has just finished the last dreaming story for the night. When she had started the first story, she had felt a little nervous. She was used to her grandmother listening, beside her, but tonight her mother and aunt were there too.

She looks at her mother beside her, and her mother leans across and gives her a side squeeze. Her voice seems to tremble when she says, "I'm so proud of you." Libby looks into her eyes to see tears forming.

"Oh, thanks Mum," she says, giving her a much relieved smile.

"That goes for me too," Aunt Grace says, leaning across Rachel, and patting Libby's leg.

"Thank you, Aunt Grace," she adds, and she leans back in her camp chair with a big sigh. She now feels very relaxed.

Some people had begun to mill around Grandma Mary, the moment Libby had finished telling the last story, but she had still taken the time to reach across and pat Libby on the leg too, affirming her approval of her story-telling.

Libby looks between the people beginning to stand, and spots Jim, where he had been standing during the story-telling. Hanna is beside him. She wants to talk to him alone. Well, there was only one way to do it.

She interrupts her mother talking to Aunt Grace.

"Mum, I'm going over there for a bit," she says, pointing to where Jim is standing. She notices Hanna is talking to him, and he is nodding, but looking in Libby's direction.

As she stands, her mother says, "That's fine darling. I'll keep an eye on Grandma."

She walks confidently around the fire, and notices that Jim hasn't taken his eyes from her. Hanna now turns to see where he is looking, and she stops talking, a frown developing.

"Hi," Libby says, looking at Jim, and ignoring Hanna.

He smiles. "Hi," he says, with a twinkle in his eye, she can't ignore, and which gives her confidence. She turns to Hanna.

"Hanna, I wonder if you'd mind - I'd like to talk to Jim alone for a bit." She looks at Jim. "If that's ok?" she asks.

He nods, and both Jim and Libby, look at Hanna. Hanna does not look at all happy, but she shrugs her shoulders and walks off.

Libby looks over towards one of the cabins and motions to the table and chairs alongside it. "Let's go and sit there," she says, not waiting for a reply, and begins to walk towards it. She feels Jim now at her side.

Once they sit, he looks inquisitively at her, but she remains silent, biting her bottom lip nervously.

Jim can feel her apprehension, so he figures he may as well get some things off his own chest.

"I guess you'll be going back tomorrow; to Dubbo." he says.

She nods. He decides he might as well come out with it.

"So, who's the lucky fella?"

She opens her eyes wide. He has obviously thrown her completely off balance.

"Oh, no, I don't have a boyfriend, if that's what you mean."

She hadn't expected that, and isn't sure she had wanted to make that clear – yet. But, it's out now, so she may as well ask her questions, so she can get them out of her head.

"What happened to Roger?"

Now it is Jim's turn to balk.

"You mean, after he…left?

"No, I mean, how long was he here for?"

"So, no one told you? Your aunt?"

"No, Aunt Grace told me to ask you. I still don't understand – why! I'm finding it quite confusing," she says, and it is apparent to Jim, by the frown on her face.

Jim is also surprised that she didn't already know, but now it made sense, why she asked him about the scar on his face. Of course, *she didn't know*!

"Well, Roger left about a week after you did, and his uncle, shortly after that."

"Oh I didn't think to ask about Mr Sutton when you told me your father was the new Property Manager. Did he leave because Aunt Grace offered your father the position?

"No..."

"Then - why?"

"Well..." he begins, but then Libby's mother appears in front of them.

"Hello Jim," Rachel says with a smile. "I'm Libby's Mum, in case you've forgotten. We met when you were younger."

Jim had stood up as soon as he had noticed her in front of them.

"Hello Mrs Rutherford. Yes, I do remember meeting you a long time ago."

"Good, good. Now, sorry to interrupt. I just wanted to tell Libby something." She looks at her daughter still sitting. "We're going now. I can see you're still catching up, so are you alright to walk back to the house? Remember, we all came in Aunt Grace's car."

Jim looks at Libby. "I can drive you home, if you like. After I make sure the fire is out."

"Oh, thanks. Yep, sounds good," she replies to Jim, then looks up at her mother.

Rachel seems delighted by what has just transpired. Exactly, as she had hoped. "Alright," she says, brightly. "Well, I'll see you later darling.

It was lovely to see you again Jim," she says, looking very satisfied.

"You too, Mrs Rutherford," Jim replies politely, and again sits, as Rachel walks away.

"So, why did Roger leave so quickly, and his uncle, soon after?" Libby immediately asks, prompting Jim to continue.

"Well, it was because of what Roger did, that they both left," he says, and looks closely at her reaction.

She nods, with eyes open wide, again prompting him.

"Ok," he says, as if giving himself permission to tell the story. "The day after you left – Monday, Roger began catching the same school bus as me, to the same school. All during that week, he ribbed me, trying to get me to react. You remember what he was like?" he asks.

"Yes!" she answers bluntly.

"Yep, well…I put up with it all week. He was really getting under my skin though. He just wouldn't stop. I felt like punching him to get him to shut up, but I couldn't do that on the school bus, or at school, or even here, because I didn't want Dad to get into trouble because of me. Besides, he was a lot bigger, and I guess that was probably the main reason. I knew, after what he did to Tiger, that he had a real mean streak." He stops, and looks down at his hands, thinking.

Libby doesn't speak or move as Jim's tells his story. Jim knows she is taking in every word.

"Anyway, on the Saturday, I went up to the cubby-house, just so I could be on my own, although I always imagined you there too when I was there.

Libby is feeling so sorry for Jim. She imagines all that he had been going through - not being able to get away from his tormentor, feeling trapped, and frustrated by not being able to do anything to protect himself. She is also feeling angry, but not just at Roger, at herself. She deserted Jim, when he needed her friendship the most. All of a sudden, her eyes fill with tears, and Jim notices.

"Hey, it's ok. I'm ok now. He left. Maybe I should stop there..." he begins, reaching over and rubbing her arm gently.

"Nooo, please, I need to hear it *all.*" she says, brushing away the tears that have fallen down her cheeks, with her fingertips. "*Please!*" she says again, almost pleading.

He sighs. "Well, he turned up at the cubby-house. He looked up at me, grinning like a maniac, and the he pulled off one of the branches and started smashing up the cubby-house. He started saying horrible things about Barons Reach and..." He stops, reconsidering the next words he was about to say..."

"All of it please Jim," Libby says, firmly. He can feel her anger now. Good, he thinks, better she be angry then upset. He continues. "...he said that Barons Reach was just full of abo's and abo lover's, and getting rid of me would be a good way to start to fix it."

Libby gasps, and her eyes open wide in shock, but she remains silent.

"I lost it then..." he says, and pauses. "...I wanted him to stop wrecking our cubby house but more than anything I wanted to punch him in the face to wipe that grin off his face, and stop those words he was saying. But, even though I got down the tree faster than I ever had before, by the time I reached the ground, he had already set fire to the branches around the base of the tree.

"Oh, so that's why it looks different now," she says, and he nods, now knowing she has now been to the cubby house recently.

"But, what happened then?" she asks softly, her anger now replaced with concern.

"I jumped on top of him, and punched him in the face."

He looks at Libby, and for the first time since he began telling the story, she notices an expression other than distaste on his face - a small sign of satisfaction. And she is pleased.

"Good!" she says, and nods. He nods back, in mutual understanding.

He sighs again. "But he got the better of me. He pushed me off, reached for that stick he always seemed to have, and swung it at me while he got to his feet. I managed to dodge it a few times, as he kept swinging, but it just seemed to make him swing harder. I wanted him to go away, so I could put out the fire, but he wouldn't stop swinging that damn stick. Anyway, he got me. Right here," he says, pointing to the small scar under his eye. "Then my eye started to hurt, and he looked at me strangely, stopped swinging the stick, and ran off. I think he reckoned he'd done enough damage when he saw all the blood running down my face."

"Oh Jim, I'm so, so, sorry," she says, and she reaches out and puts her hand on his arm.

He reaches over with his other hand and places it on hers. "Yeah, well, I tried to put out the fire the best I could, but I could see I wasn't getting anywhere, so I ran like mad to find Dad. I didn't want it to spread. Mr Sutton heard me yelling, from next door, and came to see what was going on. When they saw my face, they both started asking me what had happened, but when I mentioned – fire, Mr Sutton took off in the direction I pointed. Dad told me to go up to the main house and see your aunt. She was still there. He said she would know what to do about my eye. And then he took off after Mr Sutton.

"So you needed stitches?"

"Yeah, a few. Your aunt took me straight to the hospital. The doctor said it was lucky it wasn't a bit higher up. It could have lost my eye. Your aunt knew Dad and Mr Sutton would take care of the fire. I told her everything that had happened. And, I also told her what Roger had said - about taking care of Tiger."

Jim removes his hand from hers, and she returns her hand to her lap, but he now looks intently into her eyes.

"I'm sorry it took me a week," he says, looking guilty.

"It doesn't matter Jim – honestly," she says, tears again beginning to pool in her eyes.

"So, they put out the fire. What happened then?" she asks, as she blinks in an effort to stop her tears.

"Your aunt told Mr Sutton that Roger had to leave Barons Reach, and she told Dad that she was so upset by what he had done, she was considering calling the police. Dad told her it wasn't necessary, if Roger was leaving, but he said that if he even came near me again, he would deal with him, himself. He was so angry. Then, Mr Sutton said he was leaving too. He said he had been thinking about it for a while, and it had nothing to do with your aunt's decision about Roger, although he was naturally, mighty ashamed of his nephew. He just felt it was time for him to go, as well. They found the matches in Roger's pocket too, so even if they hadn't believed me, that was proof enough, as far as they were concerned."

"Unbelievable! Well, actually, it really is - believable, considering Roger, but I'm still trying to wrap my head around it all," Libby says, and looks down briefly at her hands. "To think, I left you alone, to deal with all that …" she begins

"It's all in the past Libby," he says, interrupting her. "We've both got to let it go, don't you think? Start afresh?" he asks, a tiny smile slowly growing to a wide grin, causing his dimples to show. That smile she remembers from so long ago.

"Yes, sounds *very* good to me," she answers, and her smile crinkles her eyes, causing fresh tears to fall freely down her cheeks.

Jim wipes them away with his thumbs as he cradles her head in his hands, and looks deeply into her eyes.

EPILOGUE

Libby stirs and opens her eyes, to see her aunt watching her closely.

"Oh sorry, I must have nodded off," she says.

"Well, it is a warm day dear," her aunt offers, smiling briefly at her niece, and looking back out at the hills from her seat on the verandah. Things at Barons Reach were just about to change, and she was so glad Libby had asked her to be here for the event.

Libby places one hand on her side as she struggles to stand. She notices her aunt is about to stand too.

"No, I'm fine. I can do it," she says. "I'm just going to stretch my legs for a bit. Be back soon."

"Ok, just yell if you need a hand," her aunt says, as Libby slowly walks away.

Libby enters the house and walks down the hallway, stopping at the side table resting against the wall, between the office and the library. Positioned on the wall above the side-table are several framed photographs.

Her eyes move first to her wedding photograph, and her eyes light up at the memory of that wonderful day. They had married just after her twenty-first birthday. Jim had turned twenty-one a few months before.

Some people said it had been a very short courtship, that they hadn't known each other very long. But for those who knew them well, as far as they were concerned, they had loved each other nearly all their lives.

After the night by the fire, when Libby and Jim had resolved everything they had needed to, Libby began to spend nearly every weekend at Barons Reach, even if there were no tours.

Aunt Grace had decided then, that it was time to tell her - she had already handed Murruway over to her, legally, so she could live there whenever she chose to. It was now her home! She had adjusted her Will the last time she had been to see her solicitor, so that the house was now hers, and upon her aunt's death, Barons Reach would also be hers. She said she knew Libby would choose the right man for a husband - one who would care for Murruway, and Barons Reach, as if it had always been his. She said her grandmother had known for a very long time, that one day she and Jim would be the next caretakers.

Libby left her job at the Council in Dubbo, after obtaining a similar role at the Bathurst Council. She moved out of the unit she shared with Teagan, and into Murruway.

One of Teagan's work friends moved into the unit when Libby moved out, and Teagan ended her relationship with Nick. She was now in a relationship with Matt. It seemed that - opposites do sometimes attract, romantically, after all.

Libby's eyes move to another framed photo, and her smile disappears. She places her fingertips to her lips and touches her grandmother's image in the photo.

Grandma Mary passed away, a month after Libby and Jim had married. Grandpa Don, found her sitting on the grass with her back against the gum tree at the back of the Jannali homestead. It was her favourite tree, and she often sat there listening to a family of kookaburras laughing overhead.

At first, he had thought she was asleep, because he could see from the back verandah that her eyes were closed. But as he walked noisily towards her, and she remained undisturbed, he had known.

He said he had instantly thought back to how he had heard the Kookaburras raucous laughter, just as he had been going outside to ask her if she'd like a cuppa. They had seemed louder than usual. It would have been the last thing she had heard.

Everyone knew she had an affinity with the kookaburras. That they were her aboriginal totem. They had heralded her departure that day.

Libby sighs deeply, and tears begin to form in her eyes. "I miss you Grandma," she says, softly.

She feels a sudden twitch, and her hand instantly moves to a spot where she can now feel a slight bulging. She giggles, and touches the area gently. It moves and disappears.

"That's better," she says, now smiling, and her eyes are dry again. She looks back at the photo of her grandmother.

"Twins, Grandma!" she announces to the photo. "How 'bout that? It looks like Barons Reach will have story-tellers for quite a while yet."

She turns as she hears a noise at the front door. Jim strides in and reaches her in seconds. He places his arms gently around her, and looks lovingly into her eyes.

"I've finished the cubby-house. It's been updated to be able to stand very rigorous treatment now."

She laughs. "It will be a few years yet before they can use it, you know."

"That's ok, I'll just keep looking after it, until they are ready. Just like I looked after it all those years, for *you*," he says, softly, and leans in as much as her protruding belly will allow, and kisses her deeply.

AFTERWORD

Dear Reader,

I hope you have enjoyed, The Dreaming Series (Books 1 – 3). As I have mentioned in – Authors Note, at the beginning of each book: 'Although works of fiction, I have endeavoured to ensure the authenticity of all Wiradjuri (Indigenous Australian) content.'

Therefore, I feel it is important, now I have completed the last book, to provide the following *non-fiction* information, pertaining to the Wiradjuri peoples and Windradyne.

In conclusion, I have also added the Australian government's official, 'Apology to Australia's Indigenous peoples' as spoken by (former) Prime Minister Kevin Rudd MP, on February 13th 2008.

Thank you for reading my stories.
Sincerely,
~Jan.

WIRADJURI

http://heritagebathurst.com/history-matters/indigenous-history/

The Wiradjuri People are the people of the three rivers – the Wambool (Macquarie), the Calare (Lachlan) and the Murrumbidgee. They have lived in these lands and along these rivers for more than 40,000 years. The Wiradjuri are identified as a coherent group as they maintained a cycle of ceremonies that moved in a ring around the whole tribal area. This cycle led to tribal coherence despite the large occupied area. It is estimated that 12,000 spoke the Wiradjuri language prior to white settlement. Differences in dialect existed in some areas, including around Bathurst and near Albury. The Bathurst Wiradjuri was the most easterly grouping of the Wiradjuri nation. Their totem is the goanna.

The Wiradjuri lived in extended family groups of around thirty men, women and children, moving between different camp sites across their traditional lands, which covered an area of approximately 40 miles (or 64 kilometres) square.

They made periodic journeys throughout this well-watered country around the Wambool River. The Wiradjuri fished from canoes and hunted with spears and nets for duck, kangaroo, goannas, snakes, lizards, emus, possums, wallabies and waterfowl. Their food supply also included various plants, roots and vegetables.

They travelled for trade and to perform ceremonies to honour their ancestors, their dreaming and their relationship with the land.

CULTURE

The Wiradjuri lands were signposted with carved trees, which marked burial grounds. Carved trees have been found at the junction of the Macquarie and Campbell Rivers at O'Connell. (This tree can be seen on display in the Bathurst Historical Museum).

Bora rings were located on key sites like Wahlu (Mount Panorama) where initiations and other important ceremonies were held. The caretaker's cottage in McPhillamy Park, is believed to be constructed from the stones of three bora rings where, for thousands of years, the Wiradjuri held initiations and corroborees.

Stone monuments associated with men's business have also been found on Bald Hill and Mount Pleasant.

Handcrafts included woven baskets and delicately stitched and engraved possum skin cloaks, worn for protections against the colder weather.

Women also stretched out possum skins on their laps to beat out rhythms during ceremonies and dances. Traditional dances portrayed battles, hunting and the animals which were both prey and totems for the Wiradjuri. Men decorated their bodies with white paint for these dances.

The Wiradjuri shaped their landscape through controlled burning, to encourage animals into cleared grassland for better hunting.

Spears were crafted from sharpened quartz spearheads fastened to kangaroo sinews. Stone axe heads crafted from stone on the edge of the Oberon Plateau, were traded widely.

WHITE SETTLEMENT

The first encounters between the Wiradjuri and the British colonialists were recorded in the journals of Blaxland, Wentworth and Lawson's first white expedition across the Blue Mountains.

On 31 May 1813, near the Cox's River, Blaxland wrote:

"TRACES OF THE NATIVES PRESENTED THEMSELVES IN THE FIRES THEY HAD LEFT THE DAY BEFORE, AND IN THE FLOWERS OF THE HONEYSUCKLE TREE SCATTED AROUND, WHICH HAD SUPPLIED THEM WITH FOOD ... FROM THE SAVINGS AND PIECES OF SHARP STONES WHICH THEY HAD LEFT, IT WAS EVIDENT THAT THEY HAD BEEN BUSILY EMPLOYED IN SHARPENING THEIR SPEARS."

In November 1814, Assistant Surveyor George Evans and five others, surveyed a road across the mountains to access the open plains to grow food for the Port Jackson colony. They followed the Wambool (Macquarie) westward into Wiradjuri country, reaching as far as Killongbutta (approx. 40 kilometres from Bathurst). Evans' route across the mountains followed a long established route used by the Dharug and Gandangara people to trade with the Wiradjuri.

Evans remarked:

"I SAW NO MEN, BUT I HAVE REASON TO THINK FROM THE MANY DISTANT COLUMNS OF SMOKE I OCCASIONALLY OBSERVED, THE INHABITANTS ARE NUMEROUS, BESIDES I FREQUENTLY CAME UPON THEIR DESERTED CAMP GROUNDS."

The first recorded contact was near Mount Pleasant, when a small group of two women and four children were surprised to find the white men fishing at dusk, in 1813.

"THE POOR CREATURES TREMBLED AND FELL DOWN IN FRIGHT."

The Wiradjuri language gives some clue as to what they must have made of these strange pale clad creatures and their horses. The Wiradjuri words for white man and ghost are similar.

THE MACQUARIE YEARS

A small settlement was established near the junction of the Macquarie River and Queen Charlotte's Vale Creek. Govern Lachlan Macquarie and his wife, visited the site in May 1815, to mark the completion of the road and the inauguration of the town. The Governor recorded his first meeting with the Wiradjuri upon his arrival.

"WE FOUND HERE ALSO THREE MALE NATIVES AND FOUR BOYS ... THEY ARE ALL CLOTHED IN MANTLES MADE OF THE SKINS OF O'POSSUMS WHICH WERE VERY NEATLY SEWN TOGETHER AND THE OUTSIDE OF THE SKINS WERE CARVED IN A REMARKABLY NEAT MANNER. THEY APPEAR TO BE VERY INOFFENSIVE AND CLEARLY IN THEIR PERSONS."

Under Governor Macquarie, white settlement west of the mountains proceeded slowly. Land grants were restricted to east of the Macquarie River and Government controlled grazing and farming to the west. This expansion was too slow for critics of Macquarie's emancipist sympathies and Macquarie was replaced by Governor Sir Thomas Brisbane. The white population doubled from 114 in 1820, to 287 by 1921. Wiradjuri hunting grounds, food sources and sacred sites were usurped by white settlers.

WINDRADYNE

The Wiradjuri began to strike back, and conflict escalated as stations were attacked and cattle speared. Lives were lost on both sides. White settler reports in the Sydney Gazette recorded that over thirteen stockkeepers were killed by mid1824. There are no records of the Wiradjuri men, women and children killed in reported retaliatory attacks and poisoning. Wiradjuri resistance to the settlement also intensified with the strength and stature of one leader, Windradyne (Saturday) becoming legendary. In December 1823, Windradyne was put in irons for a month by the commandant of Bathurst, Major Morissett, for killing two bullocks.

"ONE OF THE CHIEFS, (NAMED SATURDAY) OF A DESPERATE TRIBE, TOOK SIX MEN TO SECURE HIM AND THEY HAD ACTUALLY TO BREAK A MUSKET OVER HIS BODY BEFORE HE YIELDED, WHICH HE DID AT LENGTH WITH BROKEN RIBS"

Major Morisset had Windradyne put in irons for a month on this occasion. As conflict came closer to the fledgling town, another report describes the shooting of Windradyne's family by a farmer on the potato fields on the banks of the Macquarie, across from the early settlement. Windradyne survived this encounter, and in May 1824, he mounted a campaign of guerrilla warfare, with attacks on several stations in the Bathurst area.

Early settler, William Suttor, described his narrow escape from the inflamed warriors, thanks to the lasting friendship he had established with the Wiradjuri. When they arrived at his hut, he was able to speak with Windradyne in Wiradjuri, and saved himself and his family. Attacks were recorded at Millah Murrah, The Mill Post and Warren Gunyah.

The killing of a Wiradjuri woman and two girls at Raineville, near O'Connell, in May 1824, led to the arrest of five stockmen. Prosecution of the case drew consternation from settlers who called for military intervention against the Wiradjuri. The accused were not convicted.

MARTIAL LAW

Governor Brisbane proclaimed Martial Law on 14 August 1824 and dispatched 75 soldiers to Bathurst, with magistrates permitted to administer summary justice.

A reward of 500 acres (203.3 ha) was offered in reward for the capture of Windradyne. Official records of engagement and losses were scant, but W.H. Suttor, one of the few settler advocates for the Wiradjuri, described their suffering at the hands of the forces assembled under Major Morisset.

"WHEN MARTIAL LAW HAD RUN ITS COURSE EXTERMINATION IS THE WORD THAT MOST APTLY DESCRIBES THE RESULT. AS THE OLD ROMAN SAID, 'THEY MADE A SOLITUDE AND CALLED IT PEACE".

Soldiers, mounted police, settlers and stockmen carried out numerous attacks on Aboriginal people. The attack continued for two months but no record of casualties was kept. By October, groups of Wiradjuri were being reported coming into Bathurst to surrender. Martial Law was repealed on 11 December 1824.

Seventeen days later, Windradyne led a group of Wiradjuri to Parramatta, where, with a dignity acknowledged by white observers, he made an entreaty for peace at the Governor's Annual Feast. On the same day, the Colonial Secretary, Early Bathurst, sent a dispatch from England, rebuking Governor Brisbane for providing insufficient justification for his declaration of martial law. Brisbane was later recalled to England.

Windradyne was reported to have been mortally wounded in a tribal fight on the Macquarie River, and to have died a few hours later on 21 March 1829, at Bathurst hospital, on the corner of Bentinck and Howick Streets. The Suttor family disputed earlier accounts of Windradyne's death and burial, claiming that he had in fact departed from Bathurst hospital to join his people at nearby Brucedale, and that he died on the property in 1835. In 1954, the Bathurst District Historical Society erected a monument beside a Wiradjuri burial mound at Brucedale, attaching a bronze plaque commemorating:

'THE RESTING PLACE OF WINDRADENE, ALIAS "SATURDAY", LAST CHIEF OF THE ABORIGINES; FIRST A TERROR, BUT LATER A FRIEND TO THE SETTLERS … A TRUE PATRIOT'.

Windradyne has become a character of national importance as a resistance hero. A suburb at Bathurst, and a student accommodation village at Charles Sturt University, Wagga Wagga, are named after him.

Windradyne's grave is listed on the State Heritage Register, and is protected through a voluntary conservation order.

DISPERSAL AND RESETTLEMENT

From the mid19th century, gold mining and free selection brought thousands of new settlers into Wiradjuri country. In the mines and on the small holdings, there was little requirement for Aboriginal labour. The Wiradjuri did play an important role in the gold rush, and the major finds of Kerr's nugget, and the Tambaroora gold field, are attributed to individual Wiradjuri. Local Wiradjuri were also among the first entrepreneurs on the Ophir gold fields, selling bark for huts, looking after horses, guiding, and providing other services.

With the loss of their hunting ground, the Wiradjuri were no longer able to live independently of the white population. Extended family groups moved between settlements along the key rivers, typically living in fringe camps outside of towns like Mudgee, Wellington and Cowra. They did however manage to retain their ceremonial life despite being closed out of their traditional bora grounds. Some of the Wiradjuri's social patterns also survived; such as seasonally moving family groupings, child rearing by relatives rather than parents, decision-making by consensus, and the resolution of conflict with reference to outside forces, such as the police.

From 1883, and onwards, 'protection' policies aimed to segregate Aboriginal people across New South Wales. The Protector of Aborigines had the power to create reserves and to force Aboriginal people to live on them. This brought pressure on local Aboriginal people to leave farming properties and fringe camps. On the Aborigines Protection Board Reserves movement, paid income, property ownership, access to education, and even marriage, were controlled by administrators.

Wiradjuri families were relocated to Missions such as Erambie at Cowra, Nanima at Wellington and Mudgee, or Reserves like the Wellington Common. Others were scattered across New South Wales. In both Aboriginal missions (which were supervised by a manager) and reserves (unsupervised) housing and health conditions were well below white standards; there was little or no transport to town, and children could be refused access to local schools and public facilities, like municipal pools. Until 1972, Wiradjuri families were also subject to government policies for the removal of children, and many children were raised in orphanages like Cootamundra Girls Home and Kinchela at Kempsey.

More on – WINDRADYNE

http://adb.anu.edu.au/biography/windradyne-13251

Windradyne (1800 – 1829) by David Andrew Roberts

This article was published in – Australian Dictionary of Biography, Supplementary Volume, (MUP), 2005

Windradyne (c.1800-1829), Aboriginal resistance leader, also known as SATURDAY, was a northern Wiradjuri man of the upper Macquarie River region, in central-western New South Wales. Emerging as a key protagonist in a period of Aboriginal-settler conflict later known as the 'Bathurst Wars', in December 1823 'Saturday' was named as an instigator of clashes between Aborigines and settlers that culminated in the death of two convict stockmen at Kinds Plains. He was arrested and imprisoned at Bathurst for one month; it was reported that six men and a severe beating with a musket were needed to secure him.

After some of the most violent frontier incidents of the period, including the killing of seven stockmen in the Wyagdon Ranges north of Bathurst, and the murder of Aboriginal women and children by settler-vigilantes near Raineville, in May 1824, Governor Brisbane placed the western district under martial law on 14 August.

The local military was increased to seventy-five troops, and the magistrates were permitted to administer summary justice. Windradyne's apparent involvement in the murder of European stockmen, resulted in a reward of 500 acres (202.3 ha) being offered for his capture. The crises subsided quickly, although the failure to capture Windradyne delayed the repeal of martial law until 11 December. Two weeks later, he and a large number of his people crossed the mountains to Parramatta to attend the annual feast there, where he was formally pardoned by Brisbane.

The *Sydney Gazette* described Saturday as - 'without doubt, the most manly black native we have ever beheld - much stouter, and more proportionable limbed' than most Aborigines, with 'a noble looking countenance, and piercing eye…calculated to impress the beholder'. Another observer throught him 'a very fine figure, very muscular…a good model for the figure of Apollo'. His sobriety and affection for his family and kinsmen were considered remarkable.

Apparently remaining camped in the domain of Parramatta for some time after the 1924 feast, Windradyne then returned to Bathurst. He declined to attend Governor Darling's feast the following year. In later years, he was intermittently reported as being involved in raids on maize crops or in clashes with settlers around Lake George. In 1828 an Aboriginal man being led to his execution for the murder of a stockman at George's Plains attempted vainly to pin the crime on the 'notorious Saturday'. Mortally wounded in a tribal fight in the Macquarie River, Windradyne died a few hours later on 21 March 1829, at Bathurst hospital, and was buried at Bathurst. Windradyne, had been closely associated with George Suttor, and his son, William Henry, who were strong advocates on behalf of Aborigines, during and after the period of martial law. Both lamented his passing in the Sydney press in April 1829. One of William Henty Suttor junior's, *Australian Stories*

Retold (1887) placed Windradyne at the scene of the Wyagdon attacks in May 1824, and described how his warriors had spared the life of the author's father.

Another Suttor tradition, aired shortly after World War II, disputed earlier accounts of Windradyne's death and burial, claiming that he had in fact departed from Bathurst hospital to join his people at nearby Brucedale, and that he died on the property.

In 1954 the Bathurst District Historical Society erected a monument beside a Wiradjuri burial mound at Brucedale, attaching a bronze plaque commemorating 'The resting place of WIndradyne, alias "Saturday", last chief of the Aborigines: first a terror, but later a friend to the settlers…A true patriot'. His death date was erroneously given as 1835.

In the twentieth century, Windradyne was transformed from a local figure, to a character of national importance as a resistance hero. A suburb at Bathurst and a student accommodation village at Charles Sturt University, Wagga Wagga, were named after him. In May 2000, his presumed resting place was put under a voluntary conservation order, the occasion celebrated by Wiradjuri descendants and the Suttor family, continuing a 180-year-old friendship, and creating a potent symbol of reconciliation.

Select Bibliography

- *Historical Records of Australia*, series 1, vol 11, p410

- W. H. Suttor, *Australian Stories Retold and Sketches of Country Life* (Bathurst, NSW, 1887)

- T.Salisbury and P. J. Gresser, *Windradyne of the Wiradjuri* (Syd, 1971)

- M, Coe, *Windradyne: A Wiradjuri Koorie* (Canb, 1989)

- *Sydney Gazette:* 8 Jan 1824, p2 - 30 Dec 1824, p2 - 20 May 1826, p3 – 2 Jan 1828, p3 – 21 Apr 1829, p3

- *Australian*, 19 Jan 1826, p3 – 4 Oct 1826

- *Sydney Monitor*, 18 Apr 1829, p2

- *Sydney Morning Herald*, 27 May 2000, p9.

APOLOGY TO AUSTRALIA'S INDIGENOUS PEOPLES

Copyright: Australian Government (australia.gov.au)

http://www.australia.gov.au/about-australia/our-country/our-people/apology-to-australias-indigenous-peoples

Title: Prime Minister Kevin Rudd, MP – Apology to Australia's Indigenous peoples.
Duration: 4 minutes, 3 seconds.
Recorded: Wednesday, February 13, 2008, 9:09am AEDT
Location: Parliament of Australia, House of Representatives – external site.
Author: Parliament of Australia – Department of Parliamentary Services – external site.

Apology Transcript:
The Speaker of the House (Hon Harry Jenkins MP): The Clerk.
The Clerk: Government business notice number 1, Motion offering an apology to Australia's Indigenous peoples.
The Speaker: Prime Minister.

Prime Minister (Hon Kevin Rudd MP):

Mr Speaker, I move:

That today we honour the Indigenous peoples of this land, the oldest continuing cultures in human history.

We reflect on their past mistreatment.

We reflect in particular on the mistreatment of those who were Stolen Generations – this blemished chapter in our nation's history.

The time has come for the nation to turn a new page in Australia's history by righting the wrongs of the past and so moving forward with confidence to the future.

We apologise for the laws and policies of successive Parliaments and governments that have inflicted profound grief, suffering and loss on these our fellow Australians.

We apologise especially for the removal of Aboriginal and Torres Strait Islander children from their families, their communities and their country.

For the pain, suffering and hurt of these Stolen Generations, their descendants and for their families left behind, we say - sorry.

To the mothers and the fathers, the brothers and the sisters, for the breaking up of families and communities, we say – sorry.

And for the indignity and degradation thus inflicted on a proud people and a proud culture, we say – sorry.

We the Parliament of Australia respectfully request that this aplogy be received in the spirit in which it is offered as part of the healing of this nation.

For the future we take heart; resolving that this new page in the history of our great continent can now be written.

We today take this step by acknowledging the past and laying claim to a future that embraces all Australians.

A future where this Parliament resolves that the injustices of the past must, never, never happen again.

A future where we harness the determination of all Australians, Indigenous and non-Indigenous, to close the gap that lies between us in life expectancy, educational achievement and economic opportunity.

A future where we embrace the possibility of new solutions to enduring problems where old approaches have failed.

A future based on mutual respect, mutual resolve and mutual responsibility.

A future where all Australians, whatever their origins, are truly equal partners, with equal opportunities and an equal stake in shaping the next chapter in the history of this great country, Australia.

******

***

*

www.ingramcontent.com/pod-product-compliance
Lightning Source LLC
Chambersburg PA
CBHW020614180626

46810CB00007B/2765